THE ANGEL OF TORIN WOODS

A BETWIXT THE SEA AND SHORE
NOVELLA

THE ANGEL OF TORIN WOODS

A Betwixt the Sea and Shore Novella

CLAIRE KOHLER

Cover by MoorBooks Design
Editing by Sarah Everest

This book is a work of fiction. Names, characters, places, and incidents are either the product of the author's imagination or are used fictitiously.

ISBN: 979-8-9855674-3-4

To the Christian Mommy Writers group:

Thank you for your generosity, kindness, and love. You're the
kind of community every writer should have.

Acknowledgments

Thank you to Jesus for giving me the energy, motivation, creativity, and endurance to put this story together. May it help those who need it.

Thank you to my family for their patience and support as I worked to make this story a reality.

Thank you to my beta readers, Dani and Amber. You really helped tighten up this story to make it even better!

I also want to give a special thank you to my ARC team. I am so grateful all their excitement and efforts to share this story. Megan Barnes, Kailey Bechtel, Anneka Bell, Carrie Bleak, Becky Briggs, Cailyn Brooks, Stephanie Cotta, Aubrey DeBaar, Hunter Duran, Erin Dydek, Natalie Ehinger, Kiana Gerhart, Susan Gist, Carla Harding, Annalise Healey, Karla Holdier, Angela R. Hughes, Ami Jacobs, Amanda Keller, Sarah Kretzer, Abigail Langton, Jennifer Macaulay, Sherry Marlowe, Iris Maya, Megan McLellan, Sara Noelle, Aaron Polish, Alexis Rippy, Sara Rosevear, Connie Schreiner, Emma Seay, Mel Seeley, Sarah Stasik, Stephanie, Erika Stohlberg, Ridaa Sultan, Summer, Tami Willard, and Sydney Winward, you are all so appreciated!

Prologue

The mad fisherman took another bite of apple pie, savoring its sweet, crunchy goodness before sipping his freshly brewed tea. The innkeeper's daughter had made it special for him since he liked to come by on Wednesdays, but Vincent knew everyone else in Everton loved her baking just as much as he did. If he hadn't come by early, it would have been gone by the time he'd arrived.

He sighed, letting his eyelids close. It may still be early for most of the village, but it was fishing season, so Vincent had been up since before daybreak. The innkeeper's daughter must have noticed his drowsiness, for she and her friend Briony Fairborn were chatting in the kitchen instead of the dining room where he now sat, leaving him alone with his thoughts.

Vincent still had a few places to go today, but no one was expecting him for a little while. *Perhaps I'll go take a nap before heading up to Torin Woods. . . .*

The door creaked as it opened, interrupting his solace. A young woman wandered inside, her expression guarded. She scanned the room as though searching for the quickest exit, then took a seat in the chair farthest from him. Long blonde hair draped over her petite frame like a cloak in which she could hide from the world, but her furtive manner put Vincent on edge. Though she looked as harmless as a dove, he got the distinct impression that it was only a front.

I better make sure she's no threat.

"Greetings, my friend." His voice was raspy, but he hoped the stranger wouldn't be put off. He flashed a warm smile, but she winced before giving him a slight nod.

Hmm. Is she just na friendly, or is she hiding something?

Vincent wasn't the most handsome fellow, what with his untamed blond curls and yellow teeth, so perhaps she simply didn't like what she saw. That, or she didn't care for the fishy odor that clung to him like a second coat.

He tried again. "Welcome to Everton Inn. You look like you could use a hot drink and a generous slice o' apple pie. Would you like me to ask Adaira to get you some?"

The woman shook her head. "Nay . . . I'd just like to sit." She spoke softly, with a strange accent unlike anything he'd ever heard before.

"Well, in that case, let me tell you a story to take yer mind off yer troubles."

Vincent was the greatest storyteller in Everton, sharing magical tales so effortlessly one might almost think he'd lived them himself. The children loved listening to them, and anytime he met a visitor, he always made a point to weave one into the conversation.

One could learn a lot about how someone listened to a story, if you only knew what to watch for.

The woman frowned, then smoothed out her lips. "If you'd like."

Vincent leaned forward. "Stories are a powerful thing. Used wisely, they can inspire someone to great and noble deeds. Used poorly, they can make us see enemies where there are none." He lifted his eyebrows. "And those are the deadliest o' all. Believe me, I know."

Her jaw tightened, almost as if she were thinking of some sad stories of her own, but then she said, "What is your name?"

"I didn' introduce myself?" Vincent rubbed the back of his neck as though embarrassed, but internally, he noted how she'd changed the subject. "My apologies. I'm Vincent McLaren, better known around these parts as 'the mad fisherman.'"

When curiosity flickered in her eyes, he knew just what story to tell her.

"There's an interesting story behind that nickname, if you'd like to hear it." He raised his eyebrows in challenge.

"Please share," the woman replied.

Vincent clapped his hands together, making his companion jump. "Excellent. In that case, make yerself comfortable. I became known as 'the mad fisherman' many years ago, back when I was just a lad o' fifteen. . . ."

Mistakes

Orkney Islands[1], 1731

Vincent's heart was in his throat as he opened the door and tiptoed inside. It was still early; everyone should be asleep. If he was very careful, he could get back to bed without anyone discovering he'd been gone.

CREAK.

He grimaced, hand clenched against the traitorous wooden door. He waited a few seconds, but when he didn't hear movement, he let out a breath and eased the door closed.

His feet padded silently over the cold stone floor, his heart racing in his chest. All he had to do was get through the main area, then he'd be at his bedroom. Ten more steps, he told himself. He'd perfected the art of getting in and out unnoticed over the years. He hadn't been caught in a very long time.

Father and Mother had been sleeping soundly when he'd left—he'd checked just to be sure. He hadn't needed to check on his older brother. The snores emanating from his room were assurance enough that Tam hadn't noticed anything amiss.

Vincent reached for the doorknob to his room, his pulse slowing.

---

[1] An archipelago in the Northern Isles of Scotland.

"So, are you going to tell me where you've been?" asked his father.

Vincent winced, then swung around with a smile.

Steven McLaren stood behind him, arms crossed and eyebrows raised.

"Father, I didn' think you'd be up yet. You weren' going out fishing today, were you?"

Steven's fingers drummed against his arms, his expression sterner than before. "Answer the question."

Vincent's smile wavered. "I just went out fer a morning stroll. Nothing like a walk to start the day in a good mood."

Father shook his head in disappointment. "Did you think I didn' know you've been sneaking out to listen to Mr. Thomson's stories?"

Vincent's answering laugh came out more nervous than he would have liked. "Mr. Thomson? I wouldn' do that. Na after you got so angry about it before . . ." He trailed off, his smile slipping off the rest of the way as he realized lying was only making things worse. He stared at the floor, so he wouldn't have to look at the judgment in his father's eyes.

"I'm sorry, Da'. I just . . . I just . . ."

"When are you going to give up this charade and take some responsibility? You left yer brother in the woods to die. There's no more to be said."

"But, Da', I really did see—"

Steven held up his hand. "Stop. Just stop. If you want to make it up to him, then just apologize. Dinna pretend you saw a monster in the woods, and dinna waste yer time listening to fairytales. Mr. Thomson is a fool, and only a fool would pay heed to what he says."

Vincent's shoulders fell, shame washing over him. *Perhaps I am a fool, na because I believe him, but because I keep looking fer answers when there are none. No one can tell me what I saw, fer no one else has ever seen anything like it.*

Flashes of Tam slipping into the ravine encroached on his thoughts. A normal morning playing in the woods transformed into the worst moment of Vincent's life. If only the fall hadn't knocked Tam out, maybe Vincent wouldn't have panicked so much he'd frozen stiff, convinced his brother was dead. He should have had the sense to go for help. Instead, he'd just stood there.

Until the beast had shown up.

Nine years later, and thinking o' that thing still sends shivers down my spine. He still couldn't believe he'd managed to outrun it. A creature with legs that long could surely have caught up to a terrified six-year-old.

Yet somehow I walked away unscathed while Tam's leg never fully recovered.

Father gripped Vincent's arm, drawing his attention back. His face remained hard, but a hint of pity shone in his eyes. Pity for the son who'd embarrassed him for the last nine years. Pity for the boy who would never be as good as his brother.

"I thought you'd be over this by now. Yer mother kept telling me you just needed a wee bit more time, but . . ." He sighed. "I'll just have to make you get past it another way."

The resignation in Father's tone sent a shiver down Vincent's spine. "What do you mean?"

"From now on, you'll be the one collecting firewood. Chopping down trees is fer the young, and the doctor says my back can' handle it anymore. I've been putting it off in the hopes you'd step up to the task on yer own, but—"

"What?" Vincent shook his head, panic descending on him like a sudden storm. "Nay, you can' send me back there. What if I see—"

"Enough, Vincent," Tam shouted as he yanked open his bedroom door. "Stop being a coward, and grow up." He ran a hand through his matted blond hair, his glare so intense Vincent felt like hiding in a corner.

"Ah, there you are, Tam." Father softened, always happier to see his elder son. "I was hoping you'd be up soon. Ready to go?"

Tam yawned. "Just as soon as I eat something." He plodded to the kitchen, purposely knocking into Vincent's shoulder as he passed.

Father turned back to his second son, shaking his head like he couldn't figure out how Vincent had turned out so poorly. "Tam's right, you know. 'Tis time you stopped being afraid o'

Torin Woods and started acting like the man yer about to be. By yer age, I was already betrothed and had my own . . ."

Vincent ignored the rest of his father's speech; he'd heard it before many times. Vincent wasn't his father, and he didn't want to be. Life was meant to be enjoyed, yet Father hardly ever even cracked a smile, let alone a laugh. Everything was serious in his eyes, and all he seemed to care about was hard work.

"Now, get going," Father finished.

Vincent shuffled to the door, catching Tam's eye as he went. The older boy looked away with a scowl and shoved a piece of bread in his mouth.

The brothers used to be close, but after the incident in the woods, Tam's attitude completely shifted. No longer was Vincent a friend to have fun with—now he was a thorn in Tam's side. He had tried to explain what had really happened many times, but Tam was so stubborn that it seemed nothing but undeniable proof would change his mind.

Vincent stepped outside and closed the door, his gaze drifting north. Torin Woods lay on the outskirts of the village, past the church and inn, far enough away to almost be forgotten most of the time—unless one was specifically looking for it. His father and brother weren't overly fond of the forest because of the memories it dredged up, but they didn't avoid it like Vincent did. He hadn't entered the woods at all since the accident. *It seems my luck has finally run out. . . .*

He shook his head. *Maybe they're right. After all, I only saw the thing fer a second. Perhaps my eyes were playing tricks on m—*

Nay, I know what I saw. Still, 'twas years ago, and no one else has seen it since. It must be long gone by now.

Vincent hefted his father's ax onto his shoulder and marched forward, praying he wasn't making the biggest mistake of his life.

An Enchanting Encounter

The sun had only just risen in the sky, its golden fingers not yet strong enough to pull back the curtain of mist hanging over the sleepy village. Vincent may have been lying about what he'd been doing earlier, but he truly did love being outside in the wee hours of the morning. When the sky was still new and pink and the birds were starting to sing, it felt like anything was possible. Even miracles.

Mr. Thomson seemed to never sleep, so Vincent often visited him to hear his tales about the magic creatures he'd supposedly encountered. The old man was forgetful and curmudgeonly, so Vincent could only get him to divulge a story when he was in the right sort of mood—which often translated to giving him a healthy dose of flattery and ale.

This morning, Mr. Thomson had shared all about the cù-sìth he'd once seen while gathering mushrooms near Loch Isla. He'd almost collected all he needed when a terrifying bark made him drop the basket in his hand. He'd looked out across the loch, straight into the eyes of death itself. With the shape of a dog but fur the color of moss, the creature had stalked around the edge of the water and stopped right in front of him. As soon as its rancid breath had reached him, though, Mr. Thomson had fainted. When he'd come to, the monster was gone.

Such tales were fascinating, but they weren't what Vincent truly wanted to hear. After his family's reactions to his own monster sighting, he had kept his encounter a secret from the rest of the village. His brother already questioned Vincent's sanity when their parents were out of earshot; it wouldn't do for everyone else to think the same.

Vincent knew what his neighbors did when they disliked someone.

A flock of migrating geese flew overhead, interrupting his musings with their incessant calls. He was almost to the forest, having passed the second-to-last home a short while back. The only house left was Drulea Cottage, which was just visible on the horizon. The morning fog clung especially hard to it, almost as if it were caught in a magic spell, which might not be far from the truth if the rumors surrounding the house's occupants were to be believed.

Vincent's steps were light as he entered the forbidding woods, his eyes scanning every which way for signs of movement. Sunlight drifted down from the gaps between the trees, casting shadows around him. Birds chirped now and again, but they provided the only sound apart from his crunching footsteps. The almost-silence was eerie. Vincent tried to tell himself he should be happy about it since it meant he was less likely to get snuck up on.

He didn't have to go far before he spotted a decent-sized birch tree that would suit his purposes nicely. He lifted his ax and swung, the blade making a deep groove in the gray bark. It was arduous work, but years spent hauling fishing nets with his father and brother had strengthened his arms and back.

The tree was just starting to snap when a strange sound reached Vincent's ears. He lost control of his swing, and the ax flew out of his hands, landing in the underbrush nearby. He barely noticed its absence, though, for he was too captivated by what he heard—a sweet song flitting through the air like butterflies. So soft it was almost imperceptible, yet more gripping than anything he'd ever heard in all his life.

He couldn't make out the song's words, but its beauty embedded itself so deeply in his soul he felt himself slipping from reality until he was utterly consumed by it, and the only thing that mattered was finding the owner of that angelic voice.

Vincent darted toward the sound, feet pounding against the ground. Whoever it was would no doubt hear him before he saw them, but he felt no fear, no anxiety, just overwhelming *need*. What he would do once he laid eyes on the singer didn't even cross his mind.

He veered to the right, passing a clearing and rocks. He ducked just in time as he went by a low-hanging branch. He was almost close enough to make out the song's words.

A twig snapped beneath his feet, echoing through the forest like an off-tune instrument interrupting a symphony.

The song died away, and a flurry of footsteps told him his singer was escaping.

"Wait. Stop!" he cried, maneuvering through the forest as quickly as he could.

When he rounded a group of boulders, the footsteps he'd been following disappeared.

"Hello? Are you there?" he called. With every step, the song loosened its grip on his soul until, at last, the fogginess in his mind fell away.

Vincent shook his head a few times, then looked around. *What in the . . . ?* Awareness brought with it a surge of panic, and he sped out of the forest, not stopping until he was back on the village road. He leaned forward with his hands on his knees, his breath coming in short bursts.

What was that? There's no way that was a human voice. . . .

Even without the song in his ears, a sliver of yearning remained, and he fought against the urge to turn around and go right back into the woods. Back into the lion's den.

An Unlikely Companion

"Tam! Tam, I have to talk to you," Vincent cried, barely able to get the words out through his panting as he skidded to a stop in the market square. He'd raced home already, hoping his father and brother were finished fishing for the day. They usually went out in the mornings, then brought their catch back home and cleaned it. Mother hadn't said anything about Vincent's lack of firewood when he'd returned, but the concerned look in her gaze had almost made him regret coming back empty-handed. He'd lost the ax, too, a fact Father wouldn't be pleased with.

Tam stood a few feet away with a group of friends while a few other villagers meandered from stall to stall. He grimaced at the interruption. "There's nothing you could possibly tell me that I want to know. I'm busy, so get out o' here." He dismissed Vincent with a flick of his wrist.

"But this is important." Vincent stepped into Tam's line of sight, blocking his path to one of the stalls—Mr. Buchanan's, who eyed the exchange with a mixture of amusement and irritation. If the brothers kept standing there, they'd deter potential customers, and Mr. Buchanan wasn't the sort to forgive easily when there was lost money involved.

Tam's response was a harsh bark of a laugh that left little room for misinterpretation. He moved past Vincent and loomed over Mr. Buchanan's vegetables, inspecting a few turnips as if he were considering purchasing them, though it was no secret Tam's pockets were emptier than a liar's promises. Many of the neighbors stopped walking, more interested in the McLarens' conflict than shopping.

When Vincent didn't leave, Tam asked in an offhand manner, "Did you get that firewood? 'Twas mighty cold last night."

Vincent leaned close enough that no one else would hear him. "I heard something when I was up there, Tam. Something na human."

His brother stiffened, then whirled around, snatching the front of Vincent's shirt in his fist. With wild eyes, he snapped, "Dinna play games with me. I'm much too old to believe yer lies anymore." He shoved Vincent to the ground, then raised his head like a snake, ready to strike again at a moment's notice.

Vincent picked himself up off the ground, ignoring the murmuring crowd. They would be the talk of the town until something more interesting came to light, perhaps another wild theory about the Fairborns or gossip about the new doctor who'd recently moved in.

"I wouldn' lie to you, Tam." He met his brother's eye, determination flaring in his voice as it rose loud enough for everyone to hear. "Na now, na ever. You may na think it, but I'm still the brother you remember. Please give me another chance. I heard someone singing in the woods, and the sound was so pure it had to be a fairy—or an angel or something. I dinna know exactly, but—"

Tam slapped him across the face. "What you dinna know is when to stop. Magical creatures dinna exist. I dinna care what you or Mr. Thomson or anyone else around here says."

Vincent touched his stinging cheek. Tam had pushed him around plenty of times, but that was usually the extent of the physical torment he put him through. Tam much preferred to pretend his younger brother no longer existed.

Right now, Vincent preferred that, too. The disgust darkening his brother's eyes was making it nearly impossible to keep from crying. It was already embarrassing enough to get slapped in front of everyone.

But he wasn't going to let this go. He couldn't, not when the brother he loved seemed like he'd all but flown out of reach. "What can I do to make you believe me?"

Tam snorted but took a moment to ponder his question. "Find that 'angel' or whatever 'twas you heard, and show it to me. Then I'll believe you. Satisfied?"

Vincent's smile broke free of its cage, chasing off the frightened grimace that had tried to steal its rightful place. Hope was alive again, warming Vincent's body from his core outward. A chance was all he needed. "Aye, Tam. I'll get yer angel. I promise."

"And how are you going to do that?" His brother's voice wavered, almost as if he were concerned. "Aren' you afraid?"

"I . . ." Vincent's forehead wrinkled. "I'm more afraid o' never making things right with you. Besides, the 'angel,' or whatever 'twas, ran off before I even caught a glimpse o' it. That means I'm na the only one who's frightened. If I go into the woods prepared, I'll be fine."

"Would you like some help with that?" asked a small voice.

Vincent turned, unsure who had spoken. The others gasped, then whispered among themselves as the most disliked girl in the village stepped out from the crowd.

Bethany Fairborn was both the daughter of an unwed mother of suspicious origins and on track to become Everton's next midwife. She was also the last person Vincent would have guessed would want to help him. With unusually dark hair and even more unusual amber eyes, she and her family were the subject of more than a few unsavory rumors. Many people claimed the Fairborns were witches—or perhaps even banished fairies—and it was considered unwise to keep company with them beyond what was necessary. However, their skill at birthing babies was unparalleled, and in a village where death was a frequent guest, the Fairborns' less-than-ideal reputation was worth putting up with.

Bethany was a few years younger than Vincent, not quite a child but certainly not a woman yet. Hints of her future beauty had just started to reveal themselves, but he was always careful not to let his gaze linger too long. It wouldn't do for anyone to notice him admiring the nuisance everyone wished they could be rid of.

Now he had no choice but to look at her since she was standing right in front of him, waiting for an answer. Her lovely black hair was windswept, as if she'd been running and hadn't had a chance to brush it. Far from unkempt, yet suggesting a wildness the uptight lass didn't normally exude. Her clothes were arranged in perfect order, as they normally were. Unlike the other children, Bethany was very particular about being neat, far more than a girl her age should be. She also differed from the others in that she refused to go anywhere without shoes. Almost everyone else in town—child and adult alike—didn't see much need for them, except in winter when it was far too easy to be frost-bitten. Perhaps she didn't want to get her feet dirty, or maybe she was simply following in her mother's footsteps since Mistress Fairborn also kept her feet covered.

Heat crept up Vincent's neck as he realized he was staring.

"I suppose you can come along," he said, his tone halfhearted as he tried to gauge the crowd's response.

"Are you sure you want her with you?" a young bairn[2] asked. "What if she puts a curse on you?"

Bethany's expression darkened, almost as if she was about to do that very thing to the lad who'd spoken, but Vincent quickly said, "If she's that powerful, then surely I'd want her help." His voice took on a dramatic flair. "After all, 'tis na every day one goes on a grand adventure such as this."

The boy lit up with excitement, as did several others who weren't so old as to have forgotten magic still lurked in the corners of the world. Vincent's stories were like that, weaving together possibility and wonder until even the most skeptical hung on his every word.

Vincent swung around to Bethany, but his smile fell flat at the defeated look on her face. She'd not said or done anything wrong, yet she'd been judged so harshly. He almost felt sorry for her, were it not for the danger that would put him in. If she

---

[2] Child.

was going to be his companion, he would have to be even more careful not to indulge such feelings.

"Well, if yer coming with me, let's get going. I want to be back before dark"—he shot his brother a defiant look—"with an angel in tow."

Silence Most Unbearable

After collecting some basic trap-setting supplies from the market—rope, sweet cakes, fresh flowers, and a few other items—Vincent was ready to face his foe. He wasn't going to be caught unaware this time. He was going to capture that creature, no matter what it took. His future with Tam depended on it.

Bethany had kept pace beside him, not commenting on his purchases, though she had raised her eyebrows when he'd asked Mrs. Dunnet for beeswax. "To protect my ears," he had explained. It was about midmorning by the time they began their trek back to the woods, and since it was only the beginning of autumn, they should have plenty of time to find the creature before the sun set.

Now that they were away from the bustling market, the silence became more noticeable. Anxiety buzzed in Vincent's mind. *Is this a bad idea?*

He glanced over at his companion several times, wondering how she seemed so comfortable, not only with the task they were undertaking but also with being alone with him. Walking together had earned them quite a few odd looks from the adults they'd passed. They weren't so old yet that it was considered inappropriate, but even Vincent had to admit it seemed suspicious.

"Will it bother yer mother that you've been out with me?" he ventured.

Bethany didn't respond at first, but the way her lips tightened made it clear she'd heard his question. "I . . . I dinna think she'll like it too much when she finds out." She didn't meet his eyes.

"I dinna want to get you into trouble. You dinna have to come with me." He tried not to sound too eager, but it was far less complicated to do this task alone. Even if she did prove an asset.

"Nay, actually I do," she replied.

Vincent's brow furrowed. "Why is that?"

She shrugged. "I need to do something fun."

Since when does Bethany Fairborn do things fer fun? As far as he knew, she was the most serious lass in the entire village. She stayed close to her mother and was always focused on what she needed to learn to become a great midwife. She didn't waste time on things that didn't align with that goal—ever.

Maybe she's finally relaxing a bit. . . . He peeked at her again, noting the no-nonsense expression on her face. He stifled a laugh. *Or maybe na.*

Could she be avoiding her mother fer some reason? It was no secret that Greta Fairborn was an erratic and unpleasant woman. She'd been overheard screaming at Bethany on several occasions over what seemed like very minor mistakes. Being her daughter must be difficult.

"Well, in that case, you might have picked the wrong companion," Vincent said in a mock-serious tone. "You may na know this, but I happen to be the least fun individual in Everton." He made his eyebrows dance, hoping he'd draw out her elusive smile.

When she didn't react, he coughed and looked away, cheeks rosy. They spent the next few minutes walking silently again—until Vincent could no longer bear it.

"So, are you looking forward to Mr. Sinclair and Mistress Martin's wedding?" Everton was such a small village that weddings were few and far between. All the lasses had been giggling about the coming festivities, imagining what it would be like when they became brides themselves. The lads, Vincent included, were more interested in the food and games that came after the ceremony. Marriage wasn't something he was ready to think about for himself yet, but surely it would get Bethany talking.

"Nay, na really."

When that was all she said, Vincent ran his tongue along his teeth, trying to think of a new topic. "Have you spent much time in Torin Woods?"

Bethany stiffened as if she hadn't expected him to still be talking to her. "I suppose as much as anyone else. Mostly just near the well."

He hummed in understanding, though he'd hoped she'd be more knowledgeable of the area since Drulea Cottage was just a stone's throw from the forest. "Have you ever seen or heard anything strange around it?"

"My grandmother said trows come out to play their fiddles near the well sometimes, but I've never seen them. Do you think one o' them could have been what you heard?"

Vincent's thoughts turned to Bethany's grandmother, Edith. He didn't recall much about her since she'd died when he was young, but he knew she was the first Fairborn to live here. She was also the first midwife, a title that had earned her a great deal of respect and goodwill—until her belly had rounded and no man had been brave enough to take responsibility for it.

That was the start of the family's long scandal, only worsening when Greta Fairborn had followed her mother's example and become an unwed mother herself. Vincent couldn't imagine what it must be like to have that kind of family history following you, already viewed as a blight before you'd even taken your first step.

He cleared his throat. "Did yer grandmother actually see a trow?"

A trace of a smile teased the corners of the girl's mouth. "Aye, she did. Said he was so ugly she would have squashed him to death, were it na fer the beautiful fiddle in his hands."

Vincent frowned.

"Anyone with a taste fer music can' be completely bad," she clarified.

"Ah . . . that seems logical."

Bethany lifted her eyes to his, her lips spreading into a real smile for the first time that day. "She was a very wise woman."

Something fluttered in Vincent's belly, a sudden desire to find out more about this peculiar lass. *How much would it hurt to get to know her a wee bit better?*

"Bethany, do you—"

The openness in her expression disappeared, replaced by the guarded look he was accustomed to. "Why dinna we start near Mary's Hill? I've heard tell that people have danced with fairies on Johnsmas[3] there."

Vincent nodded woodenly, trying to disguise his disappointment. It couldn't be that she disliked him. Everyone he met found him at least somewhat funny. Even Father on rare occasions. Perhaps he just needed to find a way to make her laugh. Humor was one of his favorite ways to keep fear at bay, and now that Torin Woods was in sight, he could certainly use a good distraction.

"Sounds like you know a lot about the magical folk around here," he said as they adjusted course to the northwest, skirting along the forest's edge where the trees were thin enough that he still felt moderately safe. "Did you ever hear Mr. Thomson's brownie[4] story?" When she shook her head, he continued, "He says that when he was a lad, a brownie lived in his home. It swept the floors every night in exchange fer a bowl o' milk left by the hearth. Well, one night, Mr. Thomson's mother forgot to leave the bowl, and the next morneen[5], the whole family woke up with their hair burned straight off. The brownie must have taken pity on his mother, fer her hair grew back quickly enough. His, on the other hand, never returned, and that's why he's bald to this very day."

Vincent glanced at his walking partner, waiting for her to giggle or at least crack a smile. It was a well-known fact that Mr. Thomson's hair had been bright red when he'd been a young man, and he hadn't gone bald until the last few years.

---

[3] Orkney's Midsummer celebration.

[4] A small Scottish fairy known for living in people's homes and doing their chores as long as properly compensated.

[5] Morning.

But instead of laughing like a normal person would have, Bethany's nose wrinkled in disgust. "I never have liked Mr. Thomson."

Vincent's shoulders fell. *Does she have no sense o' humor at all?*

He gave up trying to make conversation after that. When they reached Mary's Hill, they spread out in opposite directions, hoping to cover twice as much ground and planning to call out if they came upon anything promising. Vincent scanned the trees and grasses, but there was nothing out of the ordinary.

After a few minutes, Bethany gestured for him to come over to a spot a little ways off from where the townsfolk often lit bonfires. She'd found a perfect circle of mushrooms, a phenomenon most uncommon. And quite ominous.

Her face was tentative. "You dinna suppose . . . ?" She met his eyes for a single heartbeat, then glanced away.

Aha, here's my chance. This will make her laugh fer sure.

"I dinna suppose wha—" He gasped as he tripped forward into the ring. He let out a piercing scream and threw his hands in the air. "Nay, dinna take me!"

Bethany jumped back, a cry escaping her throat.

Until she realized Vincent was perfectly well, as evidenced by his guffaws as he rose to his feet.

"You horrid lad," she snapped, stomping over and smacking him in the shoulder several times.

He continued to laugh, unfazed by her weak blows. His amusement only served to fuel her frustration, and when she moved to strike his cheek, he caught her hand in his.

"I'm sorry," he said, doing his best to calm down. "'Twas just too good o' an opportunity—" His eyes moved to their joined hands, tingles running through his skin. He hadn't realized how small her fingers were. Much like how a fairy's must be.

Bethany pulled her hand out of his, pink coloring her cheeks. Her eyes were angry slits. "Well, next time, resist the temptation."

Vincent swallowed and rubbed his shoulder, which was surprisingly sore. "We better get back to searching."

"I dinna think we're going to find anything here. We'll have to go into the . . ." She pointed toward the forest, and Vincent's amusement trickled away. *Right. No more stalling.*

The two made their way into the woods, this time sticking close together.

The forest was as dead as a graveyard as they wandered through its southernmost section; the bird calls that had spoken of life and beauty earlier were now a distant memory. All that was left was a cold, slick feeling, like sweat that lingers long after skin has lost its heat. Vincent didn't want to look like a coward, especially not in front of this girl who would undoubtedly jump at the chance to pay him back for teasing her, so he forced himself to walk confidently.

Only after the sun had dipped so low in the sky that it had to be dinnertime did Vincent suggest they turn back.

No matter how determined he was to earn his brother's trust, he wasn't going to spend the night out here. Creatures could be lurking just out of sight, waiting to pounce when he and Bethany no longer had the light to guide them.

He whirled around, eyes filling with trees that all looked the same. A sinking feeling came into his stomach. *Was it left to get back to town?*

A Trick of the Light

Bethany hid a smirk. Vincent had proven more obstinate than she'd expected, but in the end, he'd still given up as she'd known he would. "So, you've changed yer mind, then? Yer na going to keep looking fer the thing you thought you heard?"

Please say you've given up. Please. The sooner he did, the sooner she could stop traipsing through the woods with this troublesome lad and life could go back to normal.

"I thought you said you believed me." He puckered his lips as though she'd wounded him, but underneath his joking manner, she thought she heard a trace of sincerity in his words.

"I said nothing o' the sort," she snapped, her tone cold, bordering on contemptuous. Even if she had hurt his feelings, she wasn't about to soften toward this boy. He was an annoyance and a threat—nothing more. "I merely agreed to help you search. And I have, haven' I?"

"Well, you have provided me with *riveting* conversation."

When he winked, it took everything in her not to laugh. As much as she hated it, he was rather amusing.

The humor fled his expression. "There is something I must confess though . . ."

Bethany's fingers curled at her sides. *Here it comes. A reason na to trust him, just like Mother warned.*

Vincent fiddled with his shirtsleeve, his gaze on the ground. "I'm na sure how to get out o' here."

Her hand relaxed, the anxiety lifting for a brief second before she reminded herself that he still wasn't trustworthy. His admission proved nothing, except that they were lost.

"Do you know how to . . . ?" He trailed off as she shook her head, then glanced around nervously.

She thought for a moment, then peered at the darkening sky. "I've got it! The sun sets in the west, and town is south o' the woods, so we need to go"—she pointed to the left—"that way."

Vincent's face lit up. "Oh, that's brilliant! Why didn' I think o' that?"

Bethany's cheeks warmed at the praise. Mother gave compliments sparingly, and they were usually reserved for something to do with her growing midwifery skills. She started to reply, but her tongue stuck to the roof of her mouth. *What should I say? "Thank you"? "Twas nothing special"?*

She settled for silence—that was easier. But she couldn't stop a small smile from working its way over her face.

They made their way south to the forest's edge, coming up to Loch Isla as twilight transformed it into a violet reflection of the twinkling sky, as beautiful as it was enticing. Bethany held back from getting too close for fear of losing herself in its cool depths.

It also wouldn't do for Vincent McLaren to remember all those times she'd declined when the other bairns had invited her to go swimming. Better to skirt around the loch quickly before the troublesome boy had time to think about such things.

A rustle caught her attention just as Vincent motioned for her to stop. She froze, then followed his finger to something on the other side of the loch.

Her eyes widened. *Was that a trick o' the light?* She'd been almost certain she'd seen . . . a person. Or something very similar to one. A short figure with thin arms and a loathsome face. But in the split second she'd spotted it, a light had flashed in her eyes, and by the time she'd blinked, it had disappeared.

She looked to Vincent, who held a finger to his lips. She waited, careful not to make a sound, and a few seconds later, the figure reappeared, a few feet from where it had been before.

Bethany held back a gasp. *What is that thing?* It was too small to be a human, but it had that sort of shape. It wore a shirt and trousers and carried a small bundle in its arms. She only got a quick glimpse before it darted into the woods.

Vincent moved that direction, but she grasped his shoulder.

"What are you doing?"

Trailing Danger

Vincent stared at the girl's hand in surprise, and she quickly let go. We're here to catch a creature, aren' we?" The determination in his tone surprised even him. A moment ago, he'd resigned himself to defeat, but now hope—in the form of a tiny magical creature—was scampering out of sight. He wasn't about to let it get away.

"I—" Conflict flickered in Bethany's golden eyes before she shook her head. "Nay, I dinna want to know. I just want to go home."

"And here I thought you wanted to help me."

She threw her hands in the air. "What does that have to do with anything?"

"What if that's the creature I heard this morneen?"

"It isn'."

"Yer just saying that because yer scared. You dinna know."

She winced, then let out a shaky laugh. "Yer right. I dinna know. How could I?" Her expression turned serious. "Why do you care so much about finding this thing?"

"I . . ." Tam's accident tugged at his mind, but now wasn't the time to explain. Not when his best shot at fixing things with his brother was getting away. "Come on." He grabbed her hand and led her farther up the edge of the treeline, then stepped under the thick leaves, trying to predict where the creature's path would intersect theirs. They moved slowly, so as not to frighten it off.

Until there, right near the ring of mushrooms they'd found earlier, he spotted the little creature—some kind of fairy perhaps.

Could that be the singer I've been searching fer? Its stocky build and trousers made it look male, but Vincent was sure the voice before had been female. *Even if it isn' who was singing, maybe it can point us in the right direction. It doesn' look dangerous. And if 'tis a brownie like the one from Mr. Thomson's story, it might even be fairly reasonable. All I need to do is a—*

Just as he opened his mouth to call out a greeting, the creature stepped into the ring and winked out of existence.

Vincent gaped, then turned to his companion. "Did you see that?"

Bethany seemed as shocked as he was, and the only response she gave was a slight nod.

"Amazing . . ." He marched up to the circle for a closer look. "I stepped into this earlier, but nothing happened. Did it na work because I'm human?" He spun around, so he could watch Bethany's reaction as he started walking backward.

"What are you doing?" Her hand quivered at her side as if she wanted to reach toward him but was holding herself back.

"Relax. Yer as jumpy as a wee moppy[6]. We already know it doesn'—" He cut off as his foot touched down inside the circle, a jolt shooting through him. "Bethany, I—"

Before he could finish, the scene before him vanished, and a new one took its place. He fell onto his backside, shaking his head a few times. He blinked, then blinked again, trying to make sense of his surroundings. *Where's Mary's Hill? Those trees dinna look familiar. . . .*

"Vincent, are you all right?" asked a voice at his side.

He lurched away, a scream in his throat, but his cheeks flamed up as he realized it was only Bethany. "Oh, 'tis you. I thought . . ." He trailed off with a self-deprecating laugh. "I dinna really know what I thought."

She rolled her eyes. "Here." She reached down to help him stand.

---

[6] Rabbit.

He took her hand gratefully, then surveyed the unfamiliar glade they now stood in. Thick grass and flowers covered the mostly circular field, but all of it was enclosed by a dense, dark forest. The only way out by foot appeared to be a well-trodden path that disappeared into the woods, though where it led was anyone's guess. "Did we just— Do you think we're in . . . ?" He couldn't say it aloud.

"I believe so. Somehow we've crossed over into the Fairy Realm." Bethany's voice shook, but she kept her expression flat.

Vincent stepped out of the ring, pulling Bethany along with him.

"What are you doing?" Her voice was even more strained now. As if she were just barely clinging to her sense of control.

"Just getting a better look around. Aren' you the least bit curious?"

She pulled her hand out of his grip. "Na at all."

Vincent took a few steps, noting the remains of several bonfires scattered throughout the grass. It reminded him of Mary's Hill back home, the place where everyone gathered for festivals and weddings. *Except I doubt whoever lit these fires was human. . . .*

He gulped, then forced himself to chuckle. "I should tell Mr. Thomson about this when we get back. 'We followed a brownie through a ring o' mushrooms and ended up in the Fairy Realm.' Do you think he'll believe me?" He gave her a lopsided grin, but she scowled in return.

"Dinna you take anything seriously? This is the Fairy Realm! We're na supposed to be here. We need to get back right now."

Vincent crossed his arms. "If yer so worried about getting back, why did you follow me through the ring in the first place?"

Her expression turned pensive. "I . . . I dinna know. I guess I just didn' want you getting into trouble."

"I get into trouble plenty. I appreciate yer concern though."

"I wasn' concerned. I—"

Footsteps stole the words from her throat. The pair looked at each other, then scrambled toward the fairy ring.

"Na so fast," said a male voice in Scots Gaelic. An unseen force yanked them back, and they toppled to the ground in a tangle of legs and arms.

"Vincent, you dunce. How could you be so clumsy?" Bethany slapped him in the shoulder as they pulled apart, making him wince.

"'Twas na me. 'Twas . . ." He fell silent at the sight of the creature standing behind them.

"O' course, 'twas you. Who else could it have—"

Vincent cleared his throat, and when she met his eye, he jerked his head toward the figure.

"'Twas me," said the short, ugly creature. It was the very thing they'd followed in here, though now Vincent realized it wasn't a brownie at all. It was a trow.

And that was infinitely more dangerous.

Caught

The creature was about three feet tall, with gray skin and a full head of black hair cropped in the same manner as the men's in town. A green shirt and trousers covered most of his body, though his hairy feet were bare. His hooked nose reminded Bethany of a bird's beak, but it was the creature's red eyes that made her blood turn cold. Eyes that seemed to see right through her facade.

Does he know what I really am? Her toes instinctively curled inside her shoes.

"So?" The creature raised an eyebrow, his gaze darting between them. "Are you going to tell me what yer doing here willingly, or am I going to have to pry it out o' you?"

Bethany trembled, too frightened to answer.

Vincent, as she might have guessed, had no such qualms. "We just happened upon it. We got lost, you see, and—"

The creature raised his finger, cutting the babbling boy off. "Nay, try again. You and all the other bairns in Everton know better than to go traipsing off into the woods at night. Were you planning to capture me, so you could show all yer friends how you snagged a trow? Well, what say you, young Mr. McLaren?"

Vincent gasped. "You . . . you know me?"

The trow rolled his eyes as if Vincent were the stupidest being he'd ever crossed paths with. Which, now that Bethany thought about it, might be the case.

I better take care o' this.

"'Twas a dare to cross over into the Fairy Realm, sir. Vincent was foolish enough to agree to it, and when we spotted you by Loch Isla, he was sure you'd lead us here. I just tagged along to make sure he didn' harm himself."

"Hey!" Vincent crossed his arms in a distinct pout. She gave him an exasperated scowl, hoping to garner the creature's sympathy. *Surely this trow has had foolish friends before, right?*

Na that Vincent and I are friends.

The creature stared at her so hard she had to look away. His expression was difficult to read. *Does he believe me? 'Tis na that far from the truth.*

When the silence stretched on, Bethany mumbled, "And now that we've successfully found our way in, we'd be very happy to leave." She hesitantly lifted her eyes, then sighed at the creature's nod.

"Aye, you better," he said, almost as if he were talking to himself. "Bringing humans to the Fairy Realm is a crime. If King Daegan finds out I led you here, he'll have me punished. You need to go right now."

"Certainly. We'll just—"

"Wait, yer na planning on hurting us?" Vincent cut in.

The trow shook his head.

Vincent sighed in relief, an irritating smile spreading over his face. "In that case, may I ask you a question?" The creature's jaw clenched, but he barreled on. "You wouldn' happen to be an enchanting singer, would you? Or maybe you know someone who is? I was out in the woods this morneen, and I heard this amazing singing. At first, I thought I was just—"

Bethany wrenched him away from the trow. "Are you seriously talking about that right now?" Her voice was an exasperated whisper.

"Listen, I know you want to go home. I do, too." At her skeptical eyebrow, he added, "'Tis just that I promised my brother I'd find that singer. Can you be patient while I find out what he—"

A chorus of footsteps sounded to their right. Bethany hadn't noticed it before, but a faint path led into the woods, illuminated by approaching firelight.

"Soldiers!" The trow grumbled what sounded like a curse, then grabbed the children's hands. "Come quickly." He pulled them in the opposite direction, stopping only once they were several feet into the forest.

"I dinna see how this is going to help," Bethany muttered. "They'll still be able to see—"

"Shh!" The trow shook his head at her, then snapped his fingers.

He and Vincent vanished into thin air.

Bethany opened her mouth to scream, but a small hand clapped over it before she could make a sound.

"Didn' I just tell you to be quiet?" The trow sounded like he was right beside her, but she couldn't see anything, except the forest. "The magic only makes you unseen, na unheard. Stay silent, or they'll catch us."

Bethany slowly nodded, though whether the trow saw the motion, she didn't know. Once his hand was off her mouth, she peeked through the trees toward the light. A group of soldiers marched forward with synchronized movements. Their silver armor gleamed, its quality grander than anything she'd ever seen before. Each figure was tall and slender, with hair in a range of colors and textures. Their expressions were all the same, somber and focused, save for the one in the front. That soldier—a black-haired male with pale skin—had suspicious eyes that scanned in all directions.

Please keep walking. Please keep walking. . . .

A Touch of Magic

The fairy held up his hand, and the soldiers stopped. He wandered away from the group, his footsteps soft as he advanced toward the trio's hiding place.

Bethany almost jumped when his gaze drifted to her despite knowing he couldn't see them. But to move at all would have been to give herself away, for his pointed ears looked like they could detect even the slightest sound. She held her breath, praying he would shift his attention elsewhere.

Another soldier called in Scots Gaelic, "Captain, did you see something?"

The leader didn't answer, his eyes still seemingly locked on her. She'd never felt more exposed in all her life. Her lungs were starting to protest the lack of oxygen, but she didn't dare take a breath. She knew from the cold, penetrating look in the fairy's gray eyes that he wouldn't hesitate to kill her as soon as she did.

Suffocation seemed infinitely better than being pierced by the long sword at his hip.

"Captain?" the second soldier asked again.

The leader finally tore his eyes away, turning to his subordinate. "Stand guard at the Veil until further notice."

The second soldier saluted him, then positioned himself in front of the fairy ring. The leader glanced toward Bethany again, then barked out an order to the others. As one, the rest of the fairies spun around and went back the way they'd come.

Once they were a safe distance away, Bethany let out her breath and slumped against the nearest tree. She'd always feared magical folk despite some of her neighbors' insistence that they weren't real. She, of all people, knew better.

But never before had she seen a fairy in the flesh. She studied the soldier at the edge of the ring, wondering how it was possible for someone to stand so perfectly still. A shiver ran through her, and when she blinked, tears trickled from her eyes. *I just want to go home. Why did I ever think this was a good idea?*

An invisible hand grabbed her wrist, but she stifled the instinctive screech rising in her chest.

The trow's voice filled her ear. "Come along a bit farther, so we can talk without being overheard."

Against her better judgment, Bethany let herself be drawn deeper into the forest. She hoped it was two other sets of footsteps she was hearing. If Vincent had been left behind—

The hand holding her let go, and both the trow and Vincent appeared in front of her. Frustration filled the trow's expression, whereas Vincent seemed more amused than anything else.

"You can talk freely here but only fer a moment while I think," the creature said. He took a few steps away from them, tapping his finger against his forehead.

Vincent nudged her shoulder. "I really thought that fairy was going to catch you fer a moment there"—

Bethany's eyes narrowed, a sharp rebuke tightening her throat.

—"but then I remembered how well you do under pressure, and I thought, 'She'll be fine.' I'm glad I was right." He winked.

The anger that had been building in her melted away, a puzzled frown forming on her face. "How do you know I do well under pressure?"

"Oh, well, anyone who can handle birthing a babe has to be good at handling pressure." He shrugged, then his face warmed with a smile. "I'm glad I'll never have to do that. I'd probably faint as soon as the mother told me the babe was coming."

"You shouldn' be talking about that. 'Tis na proper," she said sternly, ignoring the burst of pride in her heart.

"Ah, o' course, yer right." Vincent closed his mouth, but mirth twinkled in his eyes.

Bethany looked away to hide the grin twitching at her lips. *He may be an idiot, but he's kind o' charming.*

The trow whirled around with a groan. "I can' think with you two blabbing."

"Canna you just use yer magic to send us back?" Vincent's tone rang with irritation, catching Bethany by surprise. Perhaps he wasn't as oblivious to the danger around them as he acted. Maybe he was just hiding how he really felt.

But why? 'Tis completely rational to be afraid right now. There's nothing cowardly in that. I'm afraid, too—

Her eyes widened. *Is he pretending he's fine, so I will na feel as afraid?*

"Nay, I canna just 'use my magic to send you back.' I—"

"Why na?"

"Are you always this obnoxious?" The trow took a pointed step closer.

Vincent stumbled back, seeming to remember then that this wasn't a creature to be taken lightly.

"I'm so sorry, sir. He didn' mean anything by it," Bethany said, lowering her eyes in a show of respect.

The trow scoffed. "All right, yer going to need to stop calling me 'sir.' My name is Lachlan. Got it?"

Her mouth fell open. "Aren' trows supposed to be—"

"Greedy, heartless, prone to angry tirades?" he finished, a trace of humor seeping into his voice.

"And ugly—you canna forget that," Vincent added.

Bethany glared at the same time Lachlan said to her, "I see why you felt like he needed looking after."

Before Vincent could complain, the trow continued with, "There's no telling how long that guard will be at the fairy ring. And there's no way he'll let you two go through."

"How are we going to get home, then?" Bethany asked.

"You can', na until he leaves. That means you'll need to lie low here fer now."

"Lie low?" Bethany's voice rose. "But I have to get back."

"Calm down. Calm down. Do you want to bring that soldier over here?"

She winced, ashamed of herself for letting panic get the best of her. Lachlan was right: if they were going to get out of here, they would need to stay calm. "All right, fine. Then where should we go?"

"That's what I was trying to figure out," Lachlan grumbled. "Only—" Something sparked in his eyes, and he motioned for them to follow him. "This way."

Bethany readily did so, but Vincent grabbed her arm. "Are you just going to blindly trust him?"

She pulled away. "If he'd wanted to harm us, he would have by now." She poked him in the chest. "If you keep angering him, though, he may change his mind."

The two hurried to catch up with Lachlan, ducking their heads when he threw an annoyed "Shh!" over his shoulder. They crept more carefully after that, doing their best to avoid roots and fallen branches. A full moon shone above them, casting a mysterious glow everywhere its light fell. Bethany didn't want to think about how late it was.

I wonder if Mum is worried about me since I'm na home yet. . . . Nay, she's probably just angry. She glanced at the back of Vincent's head. *If she finds out I was out alone with a lad, she's going to kill me.*

The trees seemed to go on forever, much farther than the ones in Torin Woods. Bethany's legs started to burn from all the walking, and Vincent's doubts grew in her mind. *Can we trust Lachlan?*

She swallowed, then shook off the unhelpful thought.

The woods opened up to a small clearing with the largest rowan tree Bethany had ever seen at its center. Its brilliant red leaves stretched toward the heavens like tongues of flame, and clusters of small red berries nestled in its branches. She knew rowans could live over a hundred years, but this particular tree was so thick she suspected it had lived much longer.

As they got closer, Bethany's surprise gave way to astonishment. This was much more than an ordinary tree— indentations in the bark revealed a hidden door, and what she'd first thought was just a bit of lichen was actually a small window. This was someone's home.

Vincent reached up and brushed his hand through the leaves of one of the lower branches, marveling with all the wonder of a newborn seeing the world for the very first time. Bethany paused, watching his eyes light up in fascination. Even though they were in danger, even though they might not make it home, he still noticed and appreciated what was right there in front of him.

It was stupid but also strangely beautiful, such purity in the midst of chaos. She grinned despite herself, wishing she could be more like that, rather than letting fear keep her from experiencing what life had to offer.

Perhaps humans did possess a touch of magic, after all.

When they reached the door, Lachlan lifted his hand, hesitated, and then spun around. "Na a word," he warned, then whirled back and gave the door three sharp raps.

It opened to a tree on the other side.

A Disguise Most Beautiful

Wait, what's that on the bark? Vincent leaned closer to the small tree in the doorway, studying an odd shape just above its center. *It almost looks like—*

One of the branches moved to the side, revealing a grayish-brown face amidst the leaves.

Vincent wrenched the door shut before the monster could grab them, holding onto the doorknob for dear life. His head swiveled to Lachlan. "What is that thing?"

The trow closed his eyes and pressed his fingers to his temple. "Drust is na a thing." He opened his eyes and stared Vincent down, his red gaze full of reprimand. "He's a ghillie dhu, whereas you are undoubtedly the rudest human he's ever had the misfortune o' meeting."

Vincent flinched but held firmly to the doorknob. *A ghillie dhu?* He vaguely recalled mention of them in a tale or two, but he wasn't sure if they'd been good or evil.

Lachlan huffed. "You better apologize; otherwise, I *will* turn you in to King Daegan, punishment or no punishment."

Bethany elbowed him.

"I . . ." Vincent's shoulders sagged. "All right." He let go of the door and slowly pushed it open.

The ghillie dhu still stood there, but where there had been a welcoming smile before, now there was a suspicious frown.

Its limbs were long and sinuous, more tree-like than human, but now that Vincent was looking closely, he felt stupid for having mistaken them for branches. The creature's skin was the same color as tree bark, and willow leaves hung off it like feathers. The only area of its body that wasn't covered in leaves was its face, which bore two black eyes, a pointed nose, and a thin line of a mouth.

When the ghillie dhu turned to the trow, the movement sounded almost like wood creaking. "Lachlan, my friend, I wasn' expecting another visit so soon," he said, raspier than the oldest grandfather in Everton. "What have you brought me?"

"Criminals," the trow replied flatly. He checked over his shoulder. "Might we talk more inside?"

"O' course." Drust stepped aside and gestured for them to enter.

Bethany followed Lachlan, but when Vincent tried to pass through, the ghillie dhu's arm blocked his way.

"Is there something you'd care to say?" he asked pointedly.

Vincent's mouth went dry. He had no idea what ghillie dhu etiquette was. *How does one apologize to a talking tree?* "Uh . . . I'm sorry?"

Drust raised a pair of twig-like eyebrows. "Are you?"

He grimaced, feeling like a child who'd been caught eating dessert before dinner. Except, if he didn't adequately express his remorse, he might suffer far worse consequences than a slap on the hand. "Aye, I . . . I shouldn' have slammed the door in yer face. 'Tis just that—well, you were a tree—and then you weren', and . . ."

Drust laughed, the motion making his leaves rustle. "That will do. Come on in."

Vincent let out a breath of relief and followed him into his unusual home. The large open space had walls, floors, and a ceiling that resembled the inside of a tree trunk, but the wooden furniture arranged here and there neatly divided the space into a kitchen, dining area, and sitting room. A cluster of ivy hung in the back, concealing what he assumed to be a bedroom, and a string of bright yellow flowers served as the curtain for the kitchen window. Four chairs were situated around a modest table, and a purple flower sat in a vase in the middle.

"What a lovely home," Bethany said, smiling at the ghillie dhu in a way Vincent had never seen before. She'd certainly never smiled at him like that.

"Aye, lovely," Vincent echoed, though a hint of sarcasm seeped into the words.

Lachlan glared at him, and he shut his mouth, determined to keep the rest of his opinions to himself. His eyes wandered around the house as the trow quickly explained the situation to his friend, though Vincent noticed Lachlan failed to mention that they'd been following him when they'd passed through the Veil.

"What exactly are you asking fer?" Drust said once the trow had finished.

Vincent exchanged a look with Bethany as if to say, *Aye, what is he asking?*

The girl rolled her eyes and turned to the others.

"You know what will happen if they get caught," Lachlan said slowly, his expression reluctant and sheepish.

"And you know what will happen to me if I get caught harboring them."

Wait, what? Vincent opened his mouth, then hesitated when he spotted Bethany giving him a pleading look. He raised his eyebrows as if to say, *You want to stay here, then? With a tree?*

She narrowed her eyes, a storm brewing within them. Rather like Tam right before he gave his brother a beating.

Vincent held back a sigh, dropping his gaze in defeat. He'd gotten them into this mess with his impulsive actions. He owed it to her to do all he could to get them out of it. If she thought keeping his mouth shut was the best course of action, he would respect that.

For now.

Drust and Lachlan didn't seem to have noticed their silent conversation. "They couldn' have come at a worse time," the ghillie dhu said. "I still dinna understand why you need my help. Yer a trow; 'tis na like you have to use the Veil to pass between realms."

"I guess you didn' hear King Daegan's latest edict." Lachlan huffed. "In light o' recent concerns over an Unseelie invasion, all travel between realms must be on foot until further notice."

The ghillie dhu groaned. "He gets more paranoid every year." He turned to Vincent and Bethany, resignation on his bark-covered face. "You may stay with me—"

"Thank you, Drust. They—" Lachlan started to say.

"—but na looking like that." Drust extended his spindly finger toward the children.

Vincent glanced down at his clothes, then back up. "What's wrong with the way we look?"

"I can place a glamour on them to give them wings and pointed ears. They'll look like fairies," Lachlan offered.

Wings? I dinna know if I want t—

The ghillie dhu nodded, then Lachlan waved his hand, and a flash of light blinded Vincent's eyes.

After he'd blinked a few times, he stared down at himself. He didn't feel any different. "I dinna think—"

A glimmer of blue caught his attention. A pair of butterfly-like wings almost as dark as the night sky hung from Bethany's back, so long they nearly touched the floor.

Vincent's jaw dropped. *Is that what all fairies look like? She's gorgeous.*

"What? Are . . . are those wings?" The girl's voice was full of awe as she peeked at them over her shoulder. When they opened and closed a few times, she gasped. "Did I just do that? How can I do that?" She turned to Lachlan, unable to hide the excitement from her face.

The trow chuckled. "They'll move just like real ones, except dinna go trying to fly, you hear? My magic isn' that strong."

Bethany nodded and tucked a strand of hair behind her ear, pausing when her hand grazed a pointed tip. "Do yer ears look like this, too, Vincent?"

Vincent checked, a spark of alarm passing through him at the alien feeling beneath his fingers, but delight soon swallowed up his reservations. *So, this is a glamour . . . It feels so real.*

"Hmm, that's na quite right," Drust said. He rubbed his chin, then his eyes lit up. "I've got it." He pointed at Vincent and Bethany, then a green light burst from his finger.

A Promise to Keep

"What are you . . . ?" Vincent trailed off as a prickly sensation came over him. He looked down at the floor, but to his alarm, it started stretching away from him. *What is this? What's happening to me?* When the floor stopped moving, he turned to Bethany.

His heart skipped a beat. It was her, but it wasn't. The Bethany he knew was eleven winters old, not this beauty who must be at least eighteen. Sleek black hair flowed past her shoulders, contrasting with the brilliant amber of her eyes. Womanly curves had replaced her girlish figure, and her lips were temptingly full. When her eyes met his, she blushed and turned to the others.

"There we go," the ghillie dhu said, his voice humming with pride.

"What exactly did you do to us?" Bethany asked, twirling around as her wings spread out behind her.

"As protectors o' the forest, ghillie dhus are gifted at growing things. That doesn' just mean plants," Lachlan explained. He turned to Drust. "How old did you make them?"

"I gave them each ten years."

"Wow . . ." Vincent's eyebrows shot to his hairline. *I'm twenty-five now?* He admired his figure, which was much more toned than before. Then he noticed the silver wings draped across his back. He ran his fingers along the edge of one, amazed at how real it felt. So strong, yet at the same time, soft as a feather.

He grinned at Bethany, expecting her to still be as astounded as he was, but the girl's—woman's—brow knitted in confusion.

"Why did you do that?" she asked, looking from Lachlan to Drust. "Will we return to our normal ages when we go home?"

On some level, Vincent's brain told him he should also be asking clarifying questions, but he was still caught up in the magic of it all. The vision beside him was awfully distracting as well.

Vincent tugged his gaze away, wishing his heart would stop thumping so loudly. *This is Bethany Fairborn*, he reminded himself. *Even if she is the most beautiful creature I've ever seen, she's na someone I could ever like, let alone be with. Right?*

"'Tis unsafe fer you to remain as you were," Drust said. "If word reaches King Daegan's ears that two humans are in his realm, he will tear this place apart until he finds you. As fer aging you, 'tis much easier to pass you off as adults since fairy children are quite rare."

"And my other question?" Bethany asked, slightly impertinent. She didn't seem phased by whom she was speaking to. Any other girl would have been so overwhelmed by all this that she wouldn't have been able to string two sentences together.

"You'll return to yer realm exactly as you left it, and no time shall have passed," Drust promised.

"You mean, *if* we return," she corrected.

"Aye, though I shall do my best to ensure that happens." Drust's dark eyes were sympathetic and understanding in a way that seemed almost human.

Vincent looked away, slightly unnerved. Ever since the incident with Tam, he'd been afraid of the creatures in the forest. Yet Lachlan, and now Drust, were treating them so kindly he didn't know what to think anymore.

"Thank you," Bethany said, more respectfully this time.

"Now, if *yer* done interrogating my friend"—Lachlan raised an eyebrow at her—"and *yer* done admiring yerself"—he glanced pointedly at Vincent, whose attention had drifted to the muscles in his arms again—"I'd better get going."

Vincent blushed, chagrined at having been caught. Lachlan moved toward the door, but Bethany stopped him.

"How will we know when 'tis safe to leave?"

"I'll keep an eye on the border, and once the guard is gone, I'll let you know, so you two can go home," Lachlan said.

"And . . ." Bethany's voice lowered. "Are you sure we'll be safe with him?" She jerked her head toward the ghillie dhu.

Fear flickered in her eyes, revealing the inner turmoil she'd been hiding up until now. Just as Vincent recognized it, though, it disappeared again behind her cool exterior.

The trow must have noticed it, too, for his expression softened. "Drust is the keeper o' the woods here on this side o' the Veil. Anyone who stumbles into his forest, be he human or otherwise"—he paused, looking at Bethany as if to say something only she could understand—"is under his protection. And even if he wasn' the keeper, he's saved my skin a number o' times. You can trust Drust Birchide; I guarantee it."

Bethany's frown deepened as she considered his words.

"Besides, it won' be fer long, and you'll have Vincent here with you," Lachlan added. He nodded to him, his expression heavy with expectation.

Her gaze flicked to Vincent. "Oh, but he's na—" She hesitated, dismissal hovering on her tongue.

But then the doubt on her face diminished, and something else took its place—something that shocked him more than anything he'd seen all day.

Hope.

'Tis my fault we're here in the first place. Anyone else would have given up on me by now. Why haven' you?

Vincent was used to being a disappointment. He'd let his people down in so many ways over the years. He wasn't the son his father wanted. He certainly wasn't the brother Tam wanted. His friends, too, thought he was good for a laugh but not much else, as he tended not to follow through with his promises.

He tried to avoid thinking about things like that, usually drowning himself in distraction and fun, but in truth, no one had really trusted him in a long time.

But now this girl—Bethany Fairborn, of all people—was giving him another chance to be what she needed. Not someone good for a laugh, not someone to look down on, but a friend she could count on.

And in that moment, he swore to himself that that was exactly what he would be. No matter who he'd been in the past, no matter how he'd failed, things would be different this time. Finding his mysterious singer was no longer important. All he cared about now was getting Bethany home.

Conflicted

Eight weeks later

"I've got it," Vincent exclaimed, rushing up and extending a small pouch toward her.

"And yer sure this will create enough o' a distraction that we'll have time to get through the Veil?" Bethany's expression was skeptical, but her hands trembled as she reached for the pouch.

"Well, I'm na sure, but . . ."

What they'd thought would be a short stay in the Fairy Realm had turned into months of hiding out in Drust's house. The ghillie dhu had proven himself a reliable ally with a great deal of open-mindedness toward humans, but the rest of the region wasn't so trusting. The Veil had transported them to the border of the Seelie Court, a place of great beauty but also of great unrest. And with a king constantly fearful of attacks, it had proven much harder to sneak two humans across the Veil than Lachlan had predicted.

Vincent and Bethany had done their best to blend in with the native folk, even posing as Drust's new assistants when soldiers had grown suspicious of their lengthy visit. The ghillie dhu had taught them all kinds of things about caring for the forest, along with several fascinating tidbits about Seelie culture and the various creatures on this side of the Veil. But all the while, they had never given up searching for a way to escape.

"Be patient," Drust would tell them anytime they complained about their circumstances. "Lachlan will return; I know it." Then he would change the subject to the latest task he needed them to do and refuse to discuss the matter further. He was a pleasant host, which Vincent was grateful for, but he didn't seem to understand their sense of urgency. Perhaps being a ghillie dhu who'd lived hundreds of years had made the passing of time less noticeable. Indeed, he did everything at a pace that made Vincent want to scream.

That did make it easier to scheme with Bethany though, an activity Vincent was finding more and more enjoyable with each passing day. The pair usually slipped away while Drust was taking his afternoon nap, sometimes to a quiet stream a short walk from the ghillie dhu's house, other times to a meadow that used to be the home of a unicorn herd. They'd yet to go into the city since Drust claimed higher-ranking fairies would see through Lachlan's glamour and recognize them as impostors.

"Thank you fer getting this." A smile broke out over Bethany's cheeks, showing off her adorable dimples.

Vincent smiled in return, a warm feeling spreading through his chest when she touched his shoulder. Lately, it had been difficult to remember why he'd wanted to keep his distance from the beautiful midwife's daughter. The opinions of his neighbors back home felt so distant, so meaningless, he was tempted to let himself get as close to her as he truly wanted to.

A thought that sent a surge of excitement through his blood.

Today they were in the meadow amid bluebells, heather, and thistle, about to make their third escape attempt. Drust waking up in the middle of the night had ruined the first one. The second time, Vincent had accidentally broken the jar of invisibility salve they'd gotten from a nearby brownie. But now they had something far better.

If it was as effective as the redcap[7] they'd bought it from claimed, it would provide the perfect diversion for them to slip through the Veil unnoticed.

---

[7] A malevolent elf-like creature from Scottish and English folklore.

"Bethany," Vincent said slowly, "if this goes well, by morn[8], we'll be in Everton again."

She nodded, practically aglow with hope. A twinkling star shining in the darkness. He'd expected her to have given up by now, yet here she was, too stubborn to stop trying. It might have been the thing he loved most about her.

He held back a bitter laugh at the irony of all this. He never would have predicted her persistence in trying to return would be the very reason part of him wished they wouldn't.

"That means everything will go back to the way 'twas before we came here. . . ."

She cocked her head to the side, noticing the reluctance in his voice. "Is something wrong with that?"

Vincent sighed and ran a hand through his hair. He accidentally brushed his right wing, and he had to stop himself from jumping in surprise. Even after all this time, he still hadn't gotten used to those.

"I promised myself I'd get you home, and I have every intention o' doing that. 'Tis just . . ." He dropped his eyes to the ground, unable to look at her. "What if I dinna want everything to go back to the way 'twas?"

He swallowed, not sure if she'd even heard him mumble that last part.

There was a long pause, then she answered, "What are you trying to say?"

"I . . ." The truth written so plainly upon his heart refused to pass over his lips.

These last weeks, something has happened to me. Even though we're trapped here, the time I've spent with you has made me the happiest I've ever been. I dinna know if this is love, but part o' me wishes we could stay here and find out. Would you ever consider something like that?

It was selfish, far too selfish to make such a request. Even if she felt the same way about him—and that was highly unlikely—he'd be asking her to leave behind her entire life for something that might not work out.

Not to mention that they were living in hiding and at any moment, their real identities could be discovered.

---

[8] Tomorrow.

"Nothing, I was just reminiscing, I suppose." He looked around the beautiful meadow, wondering if this was the last time he'd see it. Despite its dangers, he'd grown fond of the Fairy Realm. And of the new Vincent McLaren he'd become. Unlike back home, here he wasn't constantly reminded of how much of a failure he was. While he wasn't free to be whomever he wished, he also wasn't held back by his past mistakes. He'd learned the pride of a job well done when he'd built a new home for a family of lavellans[9], whose previous lodge had been destroyed by a careless giant. He'd also become more confident after Drust had told him—for the fifth time—that he didn't know how he'd made do before Vincent had arrived.

He worried about leaving the old ghillie dhu. Drust had no family or friends, aside from Lachlan, and the trow could only visit so often. *What's going to happen to him once we're gone? Will he be able to keep up with his duties, or will he be forced to step down, so someone else can take his place?*

"There are things I'll miss, too," Bethany admitted quietly. She was staring at her hands in her lap, and her eyes held a slight sheen.

"What things?" The question burst from his lips before he could stop himself.

She let out a soft sigh, then glanced back as though she could see the ghillie dhu's home from this distance. Her mouth formed a smile, but there was no joy in it. "I've gotten rather attached to Drust"—a touch of humor came into her voice—"even if he is just a talking tree, as you say." She plucked a bluebell and held it up, watching it sway in the breeze.

Vincent watched it, too, his heart breaking a little when she opened her hand and it floated away. Their time here together felt just as fleeting.

He reached for her desperately, taking her hands in his. "Bethany, there's something I need to tell you before we do this. Just in case it goes badly."

Her golden eyes stared into his with such understanding he almost dropped her hands from embarrassment. *Am I truly that transparent?*

---

[9] Rodents from Scottish folklore said to have strong poisonous properties.

No matter. I have to say this before I lose my nerve.

He took a deep breath. "I value the friendship we've grown in our time here, but you must know I want more than that fer us."

Burning

Bethany's pulse leaped, as much from Vincent's words as the warmth of his hands. She'd known for a while that his feelings extended far beyond friendship.

She could handle his feelings. Hers were a little harder.

Ever since they'd arrived, she'd been trying to ignore them. Ignore his infectious smile, his laugh, his frustratingly sunny outlook on life. But each time she did, his light just shoved its way into her darkness even more relentlessly. Making her yearn for things she could never have.

It didn't help that Drust's magic had aged her, and what had only been a slight interest in the boy before had since bloomed into something much more unmanageable.

Not that Vincent was really a boy anymore either. He'd gone from an awkward lad with cute dimples to a man so handsome it was irksome. Between all his smoldering looks and accidental touches that sent her skin tingling, Bethany had only hoped she could last until they were back in Everton. Back to their old lives, which had overlapped only occasionally.

Now he'd made it impossible to keep pretending.

She met his eyes carefully, her face an impenetrable mask. Whatever happened, she must not let her true emotions peek through. He might be willing to drop the facade and be honest with her, but she knew being together would ruin much more than their reputations. Their very safety would be at risk.

"We can' be more than friends," she said. Her voice was steady, but her hands were weak. Too weak to pull away, too weak to deny themselves the pleasure of his skin against hers.

Please just accept this. Please let me go before I lose myself completely.

The hope in his blue eyes wavered like a candle straining against a tempest. "Why na? I know we'll be younger when we return, but I can wait."

The walls around her heart crumbled a little more. The desire to knock them down the rest of the way nearly overwhelmed her.

Do I really mean that much to him? The question scorched her lips. It was foolhardy to ask it, but she had to know—for sure. "You'd wait fer me? Even though 'twill be years?"

He nodded, his dimpled grin stretching over his face. "Time means nothing to me, so long as I know you feel the same."

The last of Bethany's resolve fluttered away, and before she could stop herself, she leaned forward and kissed him.

His lips were soft, and after his initial surprise, molded against hers with fervor. His hands moved to her shoulders, barely touching them, as if he was afraid of breaking her. Time became meaningless, cast aside in the wake of the feeling stirring in Bethany's stomach.

Is this what love feels like? She hadn't wanted to consider it, but the pounding in her heart was so loud, the fire in her veins so intense. Maybe it was, this consuming need to be close to him, to give him the same happiness she felt whenever he smiled at her.

But if she really loved him—this silly, talkative, optimistic human boy who was her complete opposite—she needed to protect him. And *she* was his greatest danger.

She pulled away and took a few steps back.

"Bethany?" Vincent opened his eyes slowly, as if in a daze, but when he saw the distance she'd placed between them, his smile vanished. "What are you . . . Are you all right?"

She shook her head, her heart rent in two. Theirs was a love that would burn them both; it didn't matter how much she wished otherwise.

"I'm sorry. I shouldn' have done that. We can'—we can' be together. Being with me would destroy you."

"After a kiss like that, you really think I'm going to let you go?" He moved forward until she was in arm's reach, but he kept his hands at his sides. "Is this about our neighbors back home? I dinna care what people will say. You shouldn' either."

Bethany raised an eyebrow. "And yer family? What about them?"

When he winced, she knew she'd struck a nerve. In all their time here, he'd barely spoken of his family. She knew his relationship with his brother was strained, and from the scene she'd witnessed in the market, she could tell he wanted to make things better between them. Declaring feelings for the village outcast certainly wouldn't help with that.

I'm sorry, Vincent, but I have no other choice.

"How much more disappointment can yer brother take?" She spoke coldly, wrinkling her nose like she was as disgusted with him as his family was.

He paled, trying—and failing—to hide the pain on his face. "Things with Tam are . . . complicated. But he'd understand once he got to know you. My parents would, too." He lifted his lips into a quivery smile as fragile as a house of cards.

One more push, and it would all crumble.

"Please, Bethany, just—"

"Why did you promise him you'd find the creature you heard in the woods?" she cut in, trying to throw him off-balance.

"What? I . . ."

"You haven' mentioned it since the night we came here. Did you just forget about it? What's Tam going to think when you go back home empty-handed?"

"Stop it!" He lifted his hands, which were now balled into fists, then turned his back on her. "If you didn' feel the same way about me, all you had to do was say so."

His shoulders were trembling, whether with pain or anger, Bethany didn't know. Her fingers ached to touch him, to smooth away their argument by admitting the truth.

But telling him would only make things worse. There was no future where they could be together. To pretend otherwise was to doom them to even more heartbreak.

You may want to be with me now, but if you knew I was the creature from the woods, you'd never forgive me.

Cornered

The night was thick with tension as Vincent and Bethany slipped into the forest. They didn't speak and hardly made eye contact, just two humans with a common interest. Not friends and certainly not more than that.

'Twas stupid to think a lass like her would be interested in me. She's ambitious and smart and hardworking, and I'm just me. . . .

Vincent wallowed in self-pity for a few more minutes, lathering it upon his broken heart like a balm until he was so miserable he almost forgot what the plan was.

A fairy guard had been stationed at the Veil night and day ever since they'd arrived, but one fairy could be dealt with. Especially if one knew how to summon a cù-sìth.

In all their time on this side of the Veil, Vincent had never actually seen one of the rare green fairy dogs reputedly as large as horses. He hoped more than ever that Mr. Thomson's stories were true, that cù-sìths were vicious, bloodthirsty, and answered to no one, not even Seelie soldiers.

Guilt welled up in his chest. *Perhaps we shouldn' do this. What if the guard can' fend it off?*

He can just fly away if he needs to, you idiot.

Bethany's hand brushed his arm, the first time she'd touched him since their argument. "Are you all right?"

He hadn't realized he'd stopped walking. He pulled away from her, not wanting to lose himself in wishful thinking. Just because she was concerned about him didn't mean she liked him. She'd made that much clear in the meadow.

"I'm fine," he answered tersely. "We're almost there. When I give the signal, you run fer it."

He barely saw her quick nod in the gathering dark, then they split off in different directions. The owls and crickets quieted as he walked; Vincent could only hope the guard wouldn't notice.

The fairy on duty tonight was unusually short, but his beautiful wings and pointed ears made his heritage obvious even from afar. Vincent barely breathed as he drew closer, keeping his body low to the ground. The trees in this forest bore thick, gnarled roots; it was easy to stumble even when you were trying not to.

The slightest misstep now would ruin everything.

Vincent stopped and slowly pulled the pouch out of his shirt. The small bag seemed perfectly harmless as it dangled from his fingers, yet its contents were supposedly deadly. The redcap had been reluctant to part with it, and he'd charged a pretty price. Vincent was glad Drust had been generous enough to give him and Bethany a percentage of his pay once they'd started working for him.

Vincent made a quick bird call, then dumped the pouch upside-down, spilling the raw meat on the ground. At the first whiff of its revolting smell, he pinched his nose to keep from vomiting. He hadn't been told what kind of meat it was, but it was definitely not something he'd encountered before. There was no way he'd forget a stench like that.

He scurried off, grimacing at the sound of his footsteps in his ears. Too loud, much too loud. But if he was lucky, the guard would stop to investigate the meat long enough for him to get away.

A deep bark made him stop dead. The cù-sìth. Fear wrapped its jaws around him, and it took everything he had to lift his eyes toward the source of the sound.

A flash of green disappearing behind a nearby tree was enough to make him race off in the opposite direction, no longer caring if anyone heard him.

How could you be so stupid! The insult slammed into Vincent's mind like a rampaging bull, gouging him over and over. *You can' outrun a fairy, but you thought you could outrun a cù-sìth?*

He leaped over the roots ahead, blood rushing through his ears. Something crashed through the woods behind him, and he didn't have to look back to know what it was.

As it closed the distance between them, he had a passing thought: *I hope Bethany made it through the Veil. I may na have been good enough to make her happy, but at least I'll have kept my promise to get her home.*

He cried out when the creature clamped onto his arm, knowing this was the end. He felt almost removed from his body as he was yanked backward. His head smacked the ground, his vision going hazy at the edges.

"Vincent, can you hear me?"

He blinked a few times, then looked to his right in amazement. Bethany hovered beside him, trying to pull him back to his feet. She had been the one behind him, not the cù-sìth, and when she'd grabbed his arm, he'd lost his balance and tumbled to the ground.

"Bethany?"

She let out a breath of relief, then tugged his arm harder. "Good, yer all right. We have to go."

Vincent jumped up, the panic in her voice reminding him of the still-present danger. The pair charged through the woods toward the Veil, hands intertwined. The trees began to thin, their target coming into view—

A piercing yelp rang through the air, and they jerked to a stop.

"Was that . . ." Bethany trailed off, then slowly turned her head as leaves crackled behind them.

Vincent swung around, placing himself between her and the threat. The fairy guard stood a short distance away, sword clenched in his hand. Even in the moonlight, Vincent could see the blood staining his blade.

The cù-sìth failed. . . and Bethany is still trapped here with me.

The cuts lining the fairy's menacing face became more noticeable as he approached, as did the large gashes on his arms and legs. His victory hadn't come easily.

"So, yer the ones who brought the cù-sìth here." The guard's tone was as sharp as the sword he wielded, and Vincent knew they should expect no mercy. Only death. Their wings and pointed ears were now a bitter sham, for their actions had made it clear what they truly were—enemies of the Seelie court. Beyond that, their identities were of no consequence.

Vincent's mind was in chaos as he tried to think of what to do. They couldn't outrun the guard and certainly couldn't fly out of here. Neither Drust nor Lachlan knew they'd left. They seemed to be out of options.

In that case—

Vincent threw up his hands, planning to barrel straight into the fairy when he least expected it. It was all he could think to do to give Bethany one last chance to get away. He glanced at her, hoping she'd understand when he jerked his chin toward the Veil. He turned back to the guard and started to lean forward.

"Vincent, stop."

He hesitated, confused at Bethany's command. "What? But—" He whirled around.

Her eyes were on him, but they held none of the fear he'd expected to find. Instead, they sparkled with resignation—and regret.

Yet a thin smile graced her pale face as she handed him something and whispered, "'Tis going to be all right. Put this in yer ears."

Exposed

Bethany tried to ignore the tremors running through her body. *'Tis going to be all right. 'Tis going to be all right.*

Her heart didn't believe it, no matter how many times she repeated the words. But she had no choice. This was the only way they were both going to walk out of here alive.

And they *were* both going to walk out of here alive. No matter how heroic Vincent wanted to be, she wasn't going to let him sacrifice himself. And she wasn't going to let fear keep her from saving the only friend she'd ever had.

Once Vincent had put the beeswax in his ears—his face still frozen in bewilderment—she stepped out from behind him and faced the guard. He was almost upon them now, sauntering forward despite his injuries. There was no urgency in his gait, for he no longer saw a threat. Just helpless mice stupid enough to be ensnared by a hungry cat.

Bethany almost felt sorry for him.

She opened her mouth and released the song that had been fluttering around her lungs ever since they'd arrived. If only she hadn't feared Vincent's reaction, they could have escaped this place ages ago. Fairies were strong, but one guard was no match for a selkie.

The fairy stiffened as her music wrapped its gentle cords around his heart, stealing away his control in an ode as sweet as death.

"Now, youthful daughter, beware o' the sea,

O' the things it can squander and steal from ye.
Beware o' promises spoken in haste,
And always keep yer heart, always keep yer heart.
High upon the rocks above the seashore,
A woman sits weeping fer memories o' yore,
O' a handsome young stranger whose strange eyes bore,
A fire so strong it made her heart soar.
Where is this stranger whom she did love?
He's gone to the sea while she weeps above.
Gone to the sea, gone to the sea,
And so she sits weeping fer her lost love."

Bethany had sung this very song the day Vincent had stumbled upon her in the woods; it was one she sang often while wandering alone, pondering the life she'd been born into. Her grandmother had first whispered the words to her mother when she'd rocked her as a babe. Then Greta had done the same for her while weeping over their cursed fate.

For though Greta had loved a human man, she'd passed on her magical blood to her daughter, dooming Bethany to the same lonely existence she led.

And now, despite all of Bethany's efforts to hide it, Vincent knew the truth. A truth with the power to ruin both her and her mother if he chose to reveal it.

She forced herself not to think about that, for she still had to deal with the fairy. She'd never tried to make someone do as she wished before. She prayed this would work.

"Forget that you saw us here," she said firmly, "then report back to yer captain and tell him you need medical attention."

The fairy turned, his sword clattering to the ground, and marched away, presumably to follow her command.

As she turned to Vincent, she almost felt like she was the one under an enchantment, for her limbs were heavier than stone. *What must he think o' me? I kept this from him, kept him from reconciling with his brother. And even worse, I shamed him fer na searching harder, all while knowing I was the one he was searching fer.*

She regretted her harsh words then—and that she hadn't told him of the love beating in her chest. Now she'd never have another chance. "We should leave." She kept her eyes on the ground, reaching for his hand.

He knocked it away.

Shattered

When the guard's malicious smile vanished and the sword fell from his hand, a funny feeling churned in Vincent's gut. His gaze swept from the fairy to the girl at his side, noting the way her mouth was moving, forming words he couldn't hear.

What's she—what's she doing? She . . . Is she— The feeling in his stomach grew as the guard inexplicably marched out of sight, but denial fought tooth and nail, desperately trying to explain away what was right before his eyes.

She couldn' be the creature I heard that day. I know her. She's my neighbor, my friend, the lass I— Her mother delivered me, fer goodness sake!

Memories hummed at the back of his mind. Rumors about the Fairborns crept through the village like ivy, but Vincent had always preferred monster stories to petty gossip. Perhaps he'd been focused on the wrong thing all these years.

He racked his brain, then random snippets emerged.

"'Twas unnatural, Bethany's birth. Greta wouldn' let anyone besides her mother into the cottage fer days, na even to bring food or gifts fer the newborn."

"They've always been too proud to ask fer help. Remember how Greta's mother, Edith, didn' talk to anyone when she first came here?"

"The other night, I heard beautiful singing on the beach, and when I went down there, Edith was sitting on the rocks."

Vincent's heart clenched. The strange, standoffish Fairborns. Now their secrecy made perfect sense.

They never were human, were they? Just pretending to be . . . Bethany slowly turned around, not meeting Vincent's gaze. She mumbled something, but he couldn't make out what it was. Shame and fear radiated off her, as if she knew just how badly she'd hurt him. As if she were human.

Then she reached for his hand.

Vincent swatted it away without thinking, his body shielding itself from a threat. "Are you going to hurt me?"

Her eyes lifted to his for the first time, brimming with unshed anguish.

Something in him shattered, the monstrous vision before him shifting back into the girl he knew. The girl he might just love. He ripped the beeswax out, ashamed of himself. *She just saved my life. How could I ask that? She may na be human, but that doesn' mean everything has been a lie, right?*

"I'm sorry, Bethany. I—"

She shook her head. "Let's just go before the magic wears off."

"Wait." He pulled her back to face him, and her gaze reluctantly met his. Betrayal and guilt mingled there in a torturous dance, each trying to dominate the other.

She looked away. "There's no time, Vincent. Whatever you want to say can wait until yer safe."

His breath caught. *Until I'm safe? What about you? Do you na think—* He dropped her wrist. "Are you afraid I'm going to tell people yer secret? You think I would do that?"

Bethany's tears were back, her voice a choked whisper as she said, "Why wouldn' you? I'm the one you've been trying to find, Vincent. I'm the one you heard singing that day. Dinna you understand that? All this time, I could have told you, but I didn'." She pressed her fingers to her heart, so overcome with emotion she almost sounded like a stranger. "And now that you know, I can' expect you to keep this quiet, na when the truth could help you make things right with yer brother. I—"

She ran off in a rush of black hair and dashed dreams.

A Hidden Key

Bethany didn't hesitate to step through the Veil, eager to leave behind both the Fairy Realm and all that had happened there. If only she could wipe away the memories as easily as she wiped away her tears. She darted through Torin Woods, determined to keep going until she was all the way home. Daybreak came and went as she ran, chasing away the darkness like a dog on a fox's heels.

When Drulea Cottage came into view, Bethany's heart leaped in her chest. She hadn't realized how much she'd missed Mother until this moment, now that they were only separated by a single door.

She touched the doorknob, then paused. *Wait, did the magic work?* She reached over her shoulder to make sure the wings were gone. When her hand grasped nothing, she let out a sigh. *Back to normal.*

Except normal is gone forever now that Vincent knows our secret. What will Mother say when she finds out?

Bethany opened the door and stepped inside, only to be met by an empty house. She slumped, partly relieved and partly disappointed that she was alone. Mother had probably gone to check on a newborn; she'd been incredibly busy lately since four women had given birth in the last month.

That gives me time to figure out what to tell her. Her legs carried her to Mother's room as she tried to gather her thoughts, but she was so drained she dropped to the floor, wishing this could all be a nightmare she'd soon wake up from.

Her gaze fell to the old chest tucked behind Mother's bed. She'd always been forbidden from opening it, but after the night she'd had, she doubted such rules mattered anymore. Not when they were about to be thrown out of town—or worse. *What's the harm?*

She threw it open, wondering what could be so important that Mother felt the need to hide it away. A few letters lay on top, along with some blankets. Bethany picked up one of the letters, skimming its contents, but the foreign words on the page baffled her. *This isn' English or Gaelic—what is it?* Someone had tried to scratch out one of the words, but she could still make it out if she stared hard. *What does cuélebre mean?*

Stumped, Bethany moved the letters and blankets aside, then froze at what she found beneath them. Something coarse and gray with a spattering of dark spots.

What is . . . ?

When she touched the material, a shiver of understanding passed through her. *This is . . . this is my sealskin!* She cradled the pelt to her breast, releasing a sharp cry. Mother had told her she'd destroyed this at Bethany's birth in a fit of anger, yet here it had lain, cold and untouched.

All this time, I thought I was trapped here, cursed to live in a village that hates me. Now Vincent is about to reveal our secret, and Mother and I will have nowhere to go. Unless . . . She turned to the window, strength flooding her weary soul.

The ocean's call, usually just a gentle thrum on her heartstrings, rose in exultation. *Yer sealskin is found,* it seemed to say. *Come to me. Find yer destiny in my waters. Leave this land o' sorrow and pain. Come home.*

Bethany hesitated. *Should I leave? Mother will be devastated if I do. I'm all she has. Maybe I—*

Mother kept this from me, another part of her argued. *Kept me from part o' myself. If I leave, perhaps Vincent will take pity on Mother and na tell. But if I stay . . .*

Bethany stood, her decision made. She'd lived her whole life as a human, following the rules Mother set, hiding the heritage she'd always wished she knew more about. Now that she held the key to unlocking all those secrets she wasn't going to put it away again.

It was time to embrace the selkie within.

Forever Changed

"Bethany!" Vincent called and called until he was hoarse, cutting through brambles and thickets as he searched for her. The girl he'd been searching for all along. But after crossing the Veil and wandering the forest for hours, he finally decided to head home.

His feet reached the familiar path he'd stood on when he'd first gone to collect firewood. It seemed so long ago now, yet to his neighbors and friends, he'd been in the market arguing with his brother just yesterday.

Except now, everything is different. The Vincent who went into the woods isn' the same one who came out. And Bethany . . .

He was still struggling to make sense of what she'd told him. They'd lived together for months, and he'd never once suspected she was the singer he'd been trying to find. To think she'd been lying to him about something so important cut him to his core.

Maybe 'tis better if things just go back to the way they were before.

Even so, he couldn't help but tenderly tuck the memories away, like a parent tucking their child in for the night. Though their time in the Fairy Realm had ended in heartache, it had also contained joy. Too much to simply cast it aside.

He hoped Drust wouldn't worry too much when he realized they were gone. Bethany had scribbled a note for him before they'd snuck out, but since Vincent was illiterate, he had no idea what she'd written for their gracious host. *Will I ever see him or Lachlan again?*

"Vincent!"

His broken heart lurched, Bethany's face filling his mind. *Did she change her mind?*

But when he looked up, Tam stood on the path directly ahead, arms crossed and expression smug. "Doesn' look like you were successful."

Vincent grimaced, but after his initial disappointment wore off, a genuine smile touched his mouth. "Hello, Tam. 'Tis good to see you." While things weren't good between them, he'd missed his older brother while he was gone. He'd lain awake many nights thinking about what he'd do when—and if—they were reunited.

He resisted the urge to hug him and simply held out his hand, but Tam snorted in disgust. "What happened to our deal?"

Heat spread up Vincent's neck. *O' course he isn' here because he wanted to see me. All he cares about is whether or na I keep my promise.* He peered into his brother's eyes, seeking even the smallest glimpse of the brother he'd lost. *Were you wishing I'd fail? Or were you secretly hoping I'd come through? Do you miss the way things used to be, too?*

After all the times Tam had ignored him, it had to mean something that he was standing here now. Perhaps some part of him believed Vincent's claims.

And I did find the angel, didn' I? She's been under our noses all along. If Tam knew what I do, he wouldn' be so hard on me anymore. He'd trust me, and we could be brothers again like before. The hope he'd clung to all these years started to solidify, no longer just a silly dream—now it could actually be real.

But something locked his jaw tight, barricading his words in his lungs.

"I can' expect you to keep this quiet, na when the truth could help you make things right with yer brother."

Bethany had been so ashamed when she'd said that—and so certain he'd expose her.

Yet she still chose to save me, anyway.

Vincent's stomach turned, all temptation to confess the truth to Tam fluttering away. To reveal Bethany's secret would mean betraying the girl he loved—something he couldn't possibly do, even if she never returned his feelings.

And he did love her—he knew that now. He'd promised himself before that he'd get her back safely, and that promise still held true now. Even if it cost him his relationship with Tam.

Father's words about responsibility flitted through his mind, and he almost laughed at the irony. Though it wasn't in the way Father had meant, Vincent felt like he finally understood what he'd been trying to teach him all these years. Being a man *was* about taking responsibility, true responsibility. And that required more than hard work—it required sacrifice.

"I couldn' find the angel," he finally said. "Sorry."

"You admit it?" Confusion lined his brother's brow.

"Aye, you were right. I guess it must have all been in my head." Vincent rubbed the back of his neck.

Tam was quiet for a moment, then chuckled, the sound dry and forced. "I'm glad you realize that."

He laughed again, but it was no less convincing. He wasn't happy about this, Vincent decided; he was unnerved. "Hmm, but it can' be good if yer hearing things that aren' there. Perhaps I should start calling you 'the *mad* fisherman.'"

Vincent shrugged. "If it makes you happy."

The twinkle that came into his brother's eye gave him a sinking feeling. He threw up his hands just as Tam wound up for a punch.

"What's the matter, Vincent? If you can admit yer mad, you should let me get in a few hits. 'Tis the least you can do after trying to convince me there was yet *another* creature in Torin Woods."

Vincent tried to sidestep around his brother, but Tam blocked him.

"Oh, yer na leaving that easily." He lowered his fist, then opened it as if he meant no harm. "I have more questions fer you. Starting with what happened today. Did you give up when you saw the trees, or did you even make it that far?" Vincent didn't answer, but Tam just kept going. "You lost yer wee friend, too. Did she wisen up and realize yer nothing but a liar? Should I go ask her how pathetic you were?"

Vincent's head flew up, his calm facade evaporating with the morning mist. *You can hurt me all you want, but yer na going anywhere near Bethany.* His voice was a dangerous rumble as he said, "Leave her out o' this."

Tam cocked his head, curious at the sudden shift. "Why? What's she going to say? Something humiliating, I hope."

Vincent gritted his teeth, trying to keep from lashing out, but Tam's mouth twisted in triumph.

"Her name is Bethany, right?" He rubbed the stubble on his chin, thinking for a moment. "She's always been a strange one. I wonder why she'd want to help someone like you. She seemed like she was at least mildly intellig—"

"I said, *leave her out o' this*." Vincent's fist came out of nowhere, slamming into his brother's jaw.

Tam fell backward, landing on the ground with a hard thump. Blood spurted from his mouth, which now hung open in a state of shock.

Vincent hovered over him, hardly recognizing himself as he growled, "You dinna talk about her like that. Na now, na ever. Do you understand me?"

The flash of fear on Tam's face—something Vincent had never been the cause of before—told him he'd gotten his point across. Vincent pulled back, then strode off, done with this. Maybe the brother he'd once known was still in there somewhere, but he wasn't going to keep searching.

He had more important things to do.

The Power of Uncertainty

As soon as the beach was clear, Bethany ducked behind a boulder and donned her sealskin. The transition was effortless, familiar, as if she'd been doing this all her life. The world dulled to black and white, but the ocean sparkled with more magic than she'd ever seen. Pure delight bubbled up inside her as she slid into its inviting arms. Instinct guided her movements as she dove under the water, twirling and flipping with the grace of a dancer.

Hours passed in moments, unnoticed in the face of such all-consuming joy. Bethany darted to and fro, exploring the underwater world of her birthright. Schools of fish scattered amongst meadows of seagrass and kelp as she passed, and crabs scuttled along on the sandy floor. And all the while, the ocean whispered in her ear, reassuring her she'd made the right choice.

Dive deeper. See the wonders below.

The seal heeded its call, pushing herself as far as she could until her lungs started crying for air, and she had to return to the surface. She did this over and over, not stopping until she was almost to the point of exhaustion.

When she finally could dive no more, she drifted along with the current, content to float wherever it took her. *What a day. I dinna think my heart has ever felt so full. I can' wait to tell Vince—*

She cut herself off, her chest suddenly hollow. *I'm sure he's told the whole village by now. What must they all be saying about me?*

Bethany could already see their disgusted faces, hear their hurtful words: *"Monster." "Cursed." "Better off dead."*

Is that what Vincent thinks o' me, too? When she'd admitted she was the mysterious singer, his face had been all too telling. Confusion followed by disbelief, then finally settling into utter betrayal. Pain emanated through her body.

Stop it, Bethany. Stop thinking about him. Focus on the sea; remember how happy you were a few minutes ago.

Yet, try as she might, the ocean no longer provided the solace it had promised, for she'd been reminded of what she'd lost—and of the deep ache in her heart.

If the sea can' fix this, what can?

Bethany glanced toward the shore for the first time since she'd left it. Though it was far away, the distance wasn't nearly as much as she'd expected. It would only take a short time to reach.

She recoiled from the thought, not wishing to shackle herself again when she had only just broken free.

But what if . . . ?

She didn't even want to ponder it, for the possibility was so slight it was almost nonexistent.

But what if? her heart repeated. *You didn' give Vincent a chance to decide how to respond once you told him the truth. How do you know he was going to betray you?*

Because Mother said that's how men are. They always disappoint you. They always let you down. Bethany's father had proven that when he'd run away as soon as Greta showed him her sealskin, disappearing before Greta had even known she was pregnant.

But this isn' yer father. This is Vincent, the boy who has been there fer you over and over. The boy you love.

Bethany shook her head, wishing she could shake off these troublesome hopes. They were foolish, and if she listened to them, she'd end up getting hurt. She was safe here in the sea and free to be herself more than she ever had been on the land. There was no good reason to return to Everton. None at all.

But what if . . . ?

With a frustrated sigh, she hauled herself back to the shore, cursing her weak heart for keeping her from the beautiful life that had been in her grasp. But she knew that "what if" would continue to torment her until she found an answer.

It wasn't until she tried to slip her sealskin back into her mother's chest that she realized she wasn't alone.

"There you are, you wicked thing."

Fury

The door slammed closed as Bethany swung around. Mother's lips were curled, her eyes blazing with fire.

"Mother?" Bethany's voice was tentative, fear shooting through her as Greta locked the door. "What are you doing?"

"You vile daughter," Mother spat. "How long have you known about the skin?"

"I . . ." Bethany stared at the pelt in her hands. *She's that upset about me finding it? But this is mine!*

Her fingers tightened around the skin, but she kept her anger in check. "I'm sorry. I only just found it today."

"Liar." Mother stepped closer, hand raised high.

Bethany squealed, lifting her arms to block her. Even so, the strike sent shock waves of pain through her left forearm. She leaned back against the bed, completely dumbfounded. Mother had never hit her before, not even during their worst arguments.

Greta gasped, throwing her hand over her mouth in horror. "Bethany, I—I'm sorry. I didn' mean to—" She shut her eyes as if that would make the reality of what she'd just done disappear.

She opened them again, shaking her head. "Nay, I know what to do." All the shame was gone now, replaced by something strange and ominous. "I should have done this years ago."

"Should have done wha—"

Mother snatched the sealskin from Bethany's grasp and made a break for the door.

"Wait, stop!" Bethany tried to grab her arm, but her mother shook her off, slipped out the door, and shoved a chair under the doorknob, trapping Bethany inside.

"Mother, let me out!" Bethany banged on the door. It wasn't the first time she'd been locked away, though the last incident had been over a year ago. *I thought we were past this. . . .*

"Why are you doing this?"

"'Tis the only way." Mother's tone was sad, broken, yet it rang with a resolve that frightened Bethany far more than her violence. Greta's mood swings were often unpredictable, but they usually only lasted a few hours. If she could just hold out, Mother would come to her senses. Probably.

"Only way fer what?" Bethany tried to lower her voice, make it as soothing as possible. Sometimes Mother could be reasoned with when she got like this, though Grandmother had always been far better at it than Bethany.

"To keep you," Greta whimpered. "Now that you've found yer skin, yer going to leave me. Just like yer father did. Just like mine."

Ah. I should have known. Bethany's heart rate slowed down. It always did come back to abandonment for Mother. *I just need to ease her fears, make her see I'm na going anywhere, then everything will be fine.*

"I already wore the skin, Mother. The ocean didn' steal me away. I'm back," she said, trying to appeal to her logical side. Facts were hard to argue with. "Why would I leave?"

"Dinna try to trick me. I know how much you hate it here."

She switched tactics. Maybe since Mother was emotional, she'd have more luck if she focused her efforts in that direction. "But yer here. Yer all I have."

And perhaps Vincent, if my stupid heart is to be trusted.

"Yer truly na going to leave?"

Bethany leaned her head against the door, relief plucking away the last few tendrils of anxiety clinging so desperately to her mind. "I promise. Now, please, let me out o' here."

There was silence for a long moment, then a soft whisper. "I wish I could believe you."

Greta's footsteps drifted away, then the front door opened and closed. *Where is she going?*

Bethany peeked out the bedroom window, hoping for a glimpse of her. At first, there was nothing promising, nothing to see, except grass, flowers, a few trees, and the road leading into town.

The smell of fire hit Bethany's nose, birthing in her such a tidal wave of fury she felt she might burst. *Nay, she can' do this!* That was when the lightning came, blinding and beautiful, giving voice to the injustice, the agony of this moment. Reunited with the other half of her soul, only to be wrenched away again forever.

She can' burn my sealskin, na when I've only just found it. Bethany fanned the rage within her, using it to fuel the storm she'd unwittingly summoned over the cottage. She whispered to the clouds, "Please rain. Douse the flames before 'tis lost forever."

Rather than a flood of water, the wind picked up, sending Bethany's pain howling through the trees even as lightning dotted the ground.

BOOM. BOOM. BOOM.

The black scorch marks left behind were a perfect match to those on her wounded soul.

I have to get out o' here. I have to stop her!

The wind changed direction, slamming into the cottage window so hard it shattered the glass. Bethany jumped back, but pinpricks of blood rose on her face and hands. She crawled through the opening, grunting when shards sliced her arms and legs, her focus solely on the escape her powers had provided.

She couldn't stop, not when Mother was outside, the skin still in her hands. The fire was struggling in the terrible gale, but Mother worked frantically to keep it lit. She stretched out her arms to toss the pelt in, then hesitated.

"Mother, give me my sealskin," Bethany roared. Her voice carried over the storm she walked fearlessly through, less human than she'd ever been.

Smothered

The storm beating against Drulea Cottage was no surprise. Everton was well-known for them, and they often blew in almost out of nowhere. Vincent had encountered far more than he could count, and he prided himself on how well he'd learned to handle himself whenever they came through. Most of Everton's squalls were over fairly quickly, but a few proved more stubborn. When a powerful one started, the trick was to get as low as possible, preferably indoors and away from anything that would easily break. Then, it was just a matter of waiting it out.

The storm he was gazing at now made him feel like a newborn—frightened, unprepared, and completely helpless. There was no rain, no hail, just shrieking wind and nearly constant lightning, striking the ground over and over to the beat of a manic drummer.

Bethany! He couldn't bear the thought that she was caught in such a tempest. Despite his fear, he charged forward, the cottage growing larger on the horizon. Smoke rose from the other side. The lightning must have started a fire.

But when Vincent came around the other side of the house, what he discovered was man-made, not from Nature's hand. Two figures stood before a small fire, the taller holding something in her hand. They seemed to be in the middle of a heated argument, oblivious to the storm swirling around them. The shorter figure—Bethany, he realized as he drew closer—

leaped in front of her mother and stretched her arms out as if to block her.

Mistress Fairborn darted around her, lifting the object in her hand. Bethany whirled around and latched onto her mother's back like a spider. *What is that she's trying to stop her from throwing in the fire? Cloth o' some kind?*

The wind continued its assault, making it nearly impossible to reach the pair. Vincent fought against it, determined to help Bethany protect whatever it was she was so desperate to save.

Mistress Fairborn stumbled, trying to shake the girl off her. Bethany held on as if her life depended on it.

"Bethany," Vincent cried, but the wind drowned out his call.

Mistress Fairborn threw her body back, catching Bethany off-guard. The girl lost her grip and tumbled to the ground, giving her mother just enough time to toss the cloth into the fire.

Bethany lunged forward, but by the time she reached it, it was too late. The fire greedily swallowed up the cloth, transforming it to ash. The wind and lightning stopped at once, the clouds turning from black to white in seconds.

Bethany glanced up at the sudden change in weather, then let out the most horrible wail Vincent had ever heard.

He wasn't far off from her now, but when she screamed, he went perfectly still, unsure what to make of all this. It almost seemed like—

That's impossible, he told himself. *How could Bethany have caused something like that?*

Yet, the way the storm had vanished as the cloth had burned was too uncanny to be a coincidence. And he already knew she was more than human.

Mistress Fairborn wandered toward her daughter, her movements wobbly and hesitant in a manner that went beyond being shaken up by the storm. As if she couldn't decide whether to comfort or condemn the girl who'd created it. She lifted her hand but stopped just before she reached Bethany's shoulder, frozen in place. Her daughter didn't seem to notice, so caught up in grief it was like she was the one who'd perished in the flames.

What kind o' loss could make her heart break like that? Something from her father?

I can' just leave her like this. He moved forward again, ready to step in where her mother had failed, but then Mistress Fairborn turned.

Vincent ducked behind the house, praying she hadn't seen him. He didn't move for several seconds, his heart hammering in his chest. Only when he heard her open the cottage's back door and slip inside did he allow himself to step out of hiding. She'd already wounded Bethany deeply; he didn't want to risk upsetting Mistress Fairborn further with his presence.

Bethany hadn't moved from her place by the fire, her moans entwining with the smoke rising in the air. Vincent's eyes swept over her, checking to make sure she hadn't been injured in the fight. Ash clung to her russet dress, turning the hem gray. Her hair was in similar condition as it hung limply about her dirt-streaked face, and her arms and legs were covered in cuts.

On an ordinary day, Vincent was sure she'd be appalled at her bedraggled state. She'd reproached him many times during their stay in the Fairy Realm for not taking better care with his appearance. Yet, right now, it seemed it was all she could do to just remain standing. Not from fatigue, per se, but there was something troubling in her eyes. Never before had they seemed so lifeless, so empty. As if the soul lighting them had been completely smothered, leaving only a shell behind.

Vincent opened his mouth to speak, then sucked in a quick breath.

One of her shoes had slipped off, revealing five webbed toes.

Light in the Darkness

Bethany's screams filled her throat, her ears, but they did nothing to fill the gaping hole in her heart. Gone. Her link to the sea and sky. Her seal form. Her powers. Gone.

All because o' Mother.

She hoped Mother could still hear her from the house, still feel the pain she'd caused. Pain Bethany would never forgive her for. *How could she do that to me? Toss away my sealskin like 'twas garbage . . . ?*

But she couldn't come up with an answer, not when she was so raw, so empty. All she could do was cry, flooding the ground with tears to make up for the rain that hadn't come and—now that she'd lost her powers—never would.

She would have continued on like that as long as she could, until the last of her energy was spent, but something blurry stepped in front of her. A lanky figure that was all too familiar.

Bethany gasped, then fell against the boy's chest, her tears soaking into his white shirt. Vincent's arms came around her slowly, then pressed her tightly to his heart.

THUMP THUMP. THUMP THUMP. THUMP THUMP.

She buried herself in the sound, his warmth, his scent. As if she could hide from the pain eating away at her.

"Shhh," he said, cradling her head in his hand. "Let's go somewhere fer a moment."

He led her away from the fire, away from Drulea Cottage, with its secrets and sorrows, away from Mother's betrayal. The pair disappeared into Torin Woods, the trees welcoming them in like an old friend. As they walked, Bethany's cries slowly died down to whimpers, her chest beginning to feel a little lighter, her body a little stronger.

And when she finally fell silent, Vincent brought them to a stop and shifted until they were standing face to face. The expression he wore was so soft and compassionate, in a way she'd never dreamed it could be after he found out the truth.

Bethany wanted to thank him for taking her away, for being kind after she'd treated him so terribly, but the words wouldn't come.

Her skin pulsed under his fingers as he wiped the moisture from her cheeks. Memories of their kiss fluttered through her mind. Their time in the Fairy Realm had been fraught with danger, yet she found herself longing for it now. Back when they'd just been Bethany and Vincent, two friends hiding how they really felt about each other. So much simpler than where they were now. There was so much she still needed to tell him, but she didn't know where to start.

"Bethany, what happened? What did yer mother do?"

The question nearly sent her spiraling into another round of sobs, but his blue eyes held her steady. She swallowed, trying to ignore the anxiety buzzing in her thoughts. *This is Vincent. If he'd wanted to hurt me, he already would have. I can trust him.*

"She . . . she burned up my sealskin," she whispered. "I'm a selkie, Vincent."

Bethany waited for him to flinch back in revulsion, but all he did was calmly nod, as if he'd already known what she was going to say.

She frowned, then repeated the words, as much for his sake as her own. The confession tasted strange on her tongue, like eating a food you used to dislike but now didn't mind. *A selkie . . .* She'd imagined telling him a thousand times, but every time she'd played out the conversation, he'd never reacted like this. He'd always run away screaming or come at her brandishing knives and nets, intent on capturing the monster he believed she was.

But neither of those scenarios matched reality. She shook her head a few times, trying to make sense of his strange, confusing response.

"I dinna understand," she said finally. "How can you na hate me? Or at least be afraid?"

Vincent cocked his head to the side as if she'd asked something silly. "Because yer still you." He took her hands in his. "Oh, Bethany, I'm so sorry about what happened. Fer—fer what you lost today."

She sniffled, but her lips tilted up into a smile. "Thank you."

"And I know you need some time to yerself after all this, but I just want you to know, I'll always be here fer you."

He squeezed her hands, then pulled her into another hug. They stood like that for so long, not saying a word, but with every second that passed, Bethany felt his light casting away the shadows on her heart.

And she started to think, *Maybe I'll get through this, after all.*

Settling Dust

Three weeks later

Bethany still hadn't approached him, and it was all Vincent could do to keep his distance. He had no one to blame but himself—he *had* told her he'd stay away until she was ready to talk. He didn't know what it was like to lose one's sealskin, but he imagined it was rather like losing an arm or leg—shocking, painful, life-altering. She needed time to work through that, or so he told himself. He didn't like that she had to stay with her dreadful mother, but he had no choice in that. In the meantime, their days returned to the way they'd been before their trip to the Fairy Realm, and their family and friends didn't seem to know the difference. Except Tam, who was more convinced than ever that Vincent had lost his mind. He even made good on his threat to start calling him "the mad fisherman," a nickname the other townsfolk found quite amusing, given Vincent's theatrical, fun-loving nature.

Vincent embraced the new title with enthusiasm, happy it kept Tam focused on him instead of Bethany. And being "mad" did come with certain perks. He was able to say far more of what he really felt without getting in trouble, and any strange behavior he exhibited tended to be overlooked.

Such as his frequent excursions to Torin Woods.

In the beginning, he wandered the forest in the hopes of "accidentally" running into Bethany, but then he started searching for a certain grumpy trow he happened to miss very much. After several days, he found Lachlan near Loch Isla, and he'd never been so happy to see someone so ugly in all his life. The trow expressed similar sentiments, though he seemed quite flustered when Vincent pulled him into a hug. He told him Drust had been beside himself for days, but other than that, the ghillie dhu was faring well.

The fairies, on the other hand, were in an uproar over a soldier who'd come stumbling to the barracks, injured and strangely forgetful. Talk of Unseelie spies had spread throughout the court, though when Vincent tried to laugh the rumors off, Lachlan pierced him with a sharp glare that told him he knew very well who was responsible for the soldier's memory loss. Vincent didn't divulge Bethany's secret, but something told him Lachlan had known about it all along.

The two of them met up often in the days after that. Lachlan showed Vincent his home in the woods, invisible to passersby, and the pair enjoyed many afternoons together, talking of the happenings in the Fairy Realm and Everton alike. Lachlan's company was soothing, despite his prickliness, for it reminded Vincent that his memories across the Veil were more than just made-up fantasies—and that he wasn't as mad as everyone else was starting to believe.

Bethany certainly wasn't helping with that. He hadn't wanted to consider it, but as the days grew into weeks, so did his doubts. Maybe she didn't want to talk to him anymore. Maybe she preferred to let the past fade into nothing.

Maybe their kiss hadn't meant as much as he thought it had.

Vincent sighed as he brought in the morning's catch, trying to get his mind off Bethany for what felt like the millionth time. He hadn't seen her in a few days, and he'd been trying not to worry. Many of the villagers had been ill lately, his father among them, so it was very possible she was feeling poorly as well. *At least Da' will be happy I caught all this herring, especially without any help.* After he'd docked and cleaned up his net, he set about gutting and scaling the fish, a task he would have enjoyed if not for the smell. Such was the life of a fisherman, a life he knew he was destined for. Tam had no skill when it came to fishing, and everyone already talked about how Vincent would be the next great fisherman of the McLaren family, even though he was the younger son.

Except now I'm the "mad fisherman," he reminded himself with a chuckle.

CREAK.

Vincent looked away from the fish, his heart nearly stopping when he saw the figure on the dock. The sun had been up for hours, but it was like dawn was breaking all over again in the gold of her eyes. *How does she get even more beautiful every time I see her?*

"Hello, Vincent," Bethany said. "May I join you?"

Holding On Tightly

Vincent stared stupidly for a few seconds before realizing what she'd asked. "Oh! O' course, though you'll likely stink o' fish if you do." He gestured to the half-gutted herring on his lap.

Undeterred, Bethany gingerly stepped onto the boat. She wobbled a bit, then regained her balance and sat down across from him. Father's boat had never felt so small. Bethany Fairborn was *here*, right here with him. All he had to do was stretch out his hand, and he'd touch her.

"You, o' all people, should know the scent o' fish does na bother me."

His pulse quickened at the coy smile on her lips. Perhaps he was imagining it; she'd never been one to tease. *And why would she after avoiding me fer so long?*

The question reminded him of his hurt, stealing the longing that had been building inside him since she'd arrived.

"Is . . . is there anything I can do fer you?" His voice shook with uncertainty, much like his trembling heart. He cleared his throat and broke eye contact, his attention returning to his task.

He stiffened when she touched his wrist. The motion was tentative, as though she feared he'd pull away, but she slipped her hand into his. "Vincent, look at me."

He couldn't have resisted even if he'd wanted to. She may have lost her selkie powers, but his heart remained under her thrall. Sparks shot between them as their gazes met, a lass with the sun in her eyes and a lad with the sea in his. Both needing each other in a way they shouldn't but needing each other just the same.

"Thank you fer waiting. And fer proving I could trust you." She swallowed, struggling with what she was trying to say. "I'm sorry I wasn' honest with you before. I was so frightened you'd tell someone . . . and that yer feelings toward me would change."

Vincent's breath hitched, his anger falling away to reveal the love he'd been trying to conceal. But now it was on full display, bursting forth from his smile, his eyes, his thumb stroking the back of her hand.

As was hers. Though she hadn't said it aloud, the delighted laugh that bubbled up from her chest was all the declaration he needed.

"You'll need to do a lot worse to make my feelings change."

There were still so many reasons why they couldn't be together, but Vincent no longer cared. He shoved the herring off his lap and leaned forward, eyelids fluttering closed.

Bethany's other hand grabbed his shoulder, blocking him from her lips. "What are you doing?"

He opened his eyes, heat spreading over his cheeks. "Kissing you?"

She smiled but shook her head. "I think you've forgotten something important."

That was very possible since it was difficult to think clearly around her.

He leaned back, then smacked himself in the forehead as the answer came to him. "Ah, I never declared my intentions, did I? Well, Bethany Fairborn, you should know I think I'm in love with you. That might sound mad, but 'tis the truth, and I fully intend to marry you as soon as—"

"We're *bairns* again." She giggled, one eyebrow raised.

Vincent winced. "I must look like such a fool right now." He rubbed the back of his neck, too embarrassed to meet her eye.

Bethany pressed her mouth to his cheek, the feather-light touch sending jolts through his skin. "I never said that was a problem. Perhaps when we're older . . ." She trailed off, her face rosy pink.

It was his turn to raise an eyebrow. "Perhaps what?"

"Dinna make me say it," she protested, covering her now-blazing cheeks.

Vincent gently pried her hands off her face. "All right, moppy, I won'."

Her expression sharpened into a scowl. "But that nickname has to die."

He laughed and swept her into an embrace. No one else in Everton might ever know it, but he held an angel in his arms, one he would do anything for.

And until she asked him to, he wasn't going to let go.

Epilogue

"So, that's the story," the mad fisherman finished with a smile. He leaned back in his seat, relishing the myriad of emotions cascading over his audience's face. Though he still didn't know her name, he'd learned plenty in the time he'd gone through his tale. Of course, he'd changed some details to protect his beloved's identity, but the story still rang with a note of truth that even the most skeptical listener would be hard-pressed to deny.

The stranger was silent for a long time. "Did you and that lass end up getting married?"

A shadow passed over Vincent's face before he could stop it. Some things hadn't turned out as he'd hoped.

"No one can know about us. Na even Briony. Agreed?"

The fisherman's chest tightened, but he pinched his lips together and ignored it. "Do you have any other questions?"

The woman frowned but accepted his refusal to answer. "What was it you saw the day your brother got hurt?"

His expression cleared. "Oh, that? You may na believe me, lass, but 'twas a dragon. Na a beithir[10]—from everything I've heard o' them, they can' fly, and what I saw had wings as big as sails." He extended his arms as far as they would go, then pointed to the left one. "And teeth as long as this."

Vincent glanced up at the stranger, expecting her to look as intrigued as she had when he'd talked of the creatures he'd

------

[10] A large Scottish serpent said to have a venomous sting.

encountered in the woods. Instead, her skin had taken on a sickly hue, her eyes wide with fear.

"Are you all right, lass?"

"Do you know what it was?" Her voice quivered like she was hanging onto her composure by a thread.

"Nay, I never did figure that out even though I've spent over a decade trying to. You wouldn' happen to know, would you?"

She swallowed, then shook her head adamantly.

Vincent wiped all the warmth off his face, trading it in for a critical glare. "Now, lass, dinna you think 'tis time you stop lying?"

"Who are you talking to out here, Mr. McLaren?" Adaira, the innkeeper's daughter, called from the kitchen. She and Briony Fairborn entered the room, teacups in hand.

When the stranger locked eyes with Briony, she gasped and fell backward out of her chair.

"Are you all right?" Adaira asked, hurrying toward her guest.

The woman shot to her feet, looking like she'd just seen a ghost. She stumbled out of the inn without a word, leaving the other three to stare after her, the first two with open mouths of astonishment and the third with a disappointed huff.

"What just happened?" Briony said.

Vincent shrugged and swallowed the rest of his tea with a loud gulp. "No idea. If you'll excuse me, ladies, I must be going now." He put some money on the table and hurried out.

Outside of the inn, the village was waking up. People emerged from their homes, ready to start the day's work. Children dashed down the streets, playing and teasing each other. Friends greeted one another with smiles and hugs. A few of the Olivers' servants hustled along the road to carry out their duties.

But the visitor was nowhere to be found.

"Hmm . . ." Vincent spun around and went on his way, not too worried about the stranger's convenient disappearance. He knew all he needed to, and as far as he was concerned, she was no threat to the people of Everton. To the residents of Torin Woods, however . . .

About The Secret of Drulea Cottage

An outcast with magical secrets. A nobleman on the run. Will the truth keep them apart?

Briony Fairborn, a midwife in eighteenth-century Scotland, comes from a family shrouded in scandal. Left with only one friend after her mother's death, she has little hope of gaining any others, let alone finding a husband. Instead, Briony tries to live a quiet life and avoid her neighbors' ridicule as much as possible.

But things in her hometown take a drastic turn when a storm brings foreigners to Everton's shore.

On the night Santiago Mendes arrives, he comes with a broken ship, a broken leg, and a broken spirit that Briony finds herself profoundly drawn to. Her scarred heart slowly starts to open, and although Briony suspects he may be hiding something, she can't help but dream of the possibility of love.

That is, until another stranger appears in town, intent on repaying a childhood debt. A dangerously handsome stranger who calls to the magic in Briony's blood. And who holds the secrets of her past.

But once the truth unravels, Briony will have to decide where her loyalties lie. Will she be Everton's salvation? Or its destruction?

Author's Note

Welcome to the world of Everton! Thank you for coming with me on this journey into an 18th-century Scotland where magic and myth lurk closer than you'd think. While this is a work of fiction, I worked hard to ensure the tone honors what life was really like in the Orkney Isles during this time period—minus the folklore, of course.

If you enjoyed Vincent and Bethany's story, please let me know by leaving a review at your preferred online retailer. These are so meaningful, especially for indie authors, and they help new readers who love my unique blend of history, fantasy, and romance get a sense of what awaits them when they pick up a copy of this story.

Join my newsletter at clairekohlerbooks.com to be among the first to know what I'll be writing next.